The Unseen Chronicles of

Amelia Black

By

A.G.R Moore

THE UNSEEN CHRONICLES OF AMELIA BLACK

By A.G.R. Moore

Print Edition | Copyright 2011 A.G.R. Moore. Cover illustration copyright © Gillian Reid.

First published in 2011.

Thank you. All of you.

You see things as they are and ask, 'Why?'

I dream of things that never were and say,

'Why not?'

George Bernard Shaw

I

ARE *you* afraid of the Dark? I often find myself asking that question to people on my travels. At one point in everyone's lives, perhaps just for a brief moment, the answer is yes. That is, until we realise there are no scary ghouls, or horrid monsters, or twisted goblins, or wretched witches lurking beneath our beds or hiding deep within our wardrobes. Those shadows and sounds are usually just our delicate, little minds playing tricks on us. After all, we always fear what cannot be seen. But what about the Unseen?

My story begins, like many before it, long ago in a land not so far away, where there lived a little girl with darling, emerald eyes and naturally deep purple hair, named Amelia Black.

Amelia was a kind, curious and wonderful soul. Just like her mother and father, Aoibhinn and Antoine {who were equally just as kind, curious and wonderful}, Amelia considered herself a great explorer of the unknown.

Being an extremely wealthy family, the Blacks lived on a great estate with a house fit for a king; or indeed a queen. Though the girl was too young to go on her parents' extraordinary adventures, she was able to hone her sense for adventure within the confines of her own home, under the watchful eye of their faithful butler and loyal friend, Julius E. Dawson {who prefers simply to be known as Dawson}.

From the cellar to the attic, from the east wing to the west wing, from the gardens to the stables, from the front door all the way to the back door. Amelia knew every hiding place within her home and where every artefact collected by her parents hid. Each day she would try to imagine herself being the one who found these treasures first; each adventure more astonishing than the last.

It was fair to say no child was ever happier, yet I fear this happiness was not to last for long. One day, one *very* tragic and painfully grey day, news broke that her mother and father had disappeared without a trace.

Amelia was all alone.

II

FILLED with great sadness from her loss, Amelia did not wish to do anything fun anymore. She would spend hours watching out her bedroom window, with the faint belief her parents would eventually appear up the long driveway of their great garden and welcome her into their arms and never let go.

However, this was not to be. And Amelia was still alone.

Many months had passed, and the mystery of the Blacks remained unsolved. No bodies, no wreckage, nothing.

"I thought I would prepare some supper..." said Dawson, solemnly.

Amelia did not respond.

"Very well..."

"Dawson," said Amelia, breaking her silence.

"Yes Ms?"

"Did they leave because of me? Because they... don't love me anymore...?" She burst into tears.

"Ms Black, I've had the pleasure of knowing your parents for many years and I can assure you there was nothing, and I mean *nothing*, on this earth – no treasure, no ancient relic, no holy grail – that they valued more than you."

Dawson himself tried to hold back the tears, for he too feared the worst of his employers. He cared for them both very much.

"I think I might just go to sleep, Dawson," said Amelia.

"Do you wish for me to tell you a bedtime story, Ms?" Dawson asked, brightly. "The Chinese Princess, perhaps? The Witches' Piper? Oh, how about, The Legend of the Troll King? You've always been fond of that one."

Amelia could tell the butler was trying his hardest, but very little could cheer her up at the minute. "No, thank you, Dawson," she replied. "You're excused."

Dawson had a slightly lost, defeatist look struck upon his face. "Very well, Ms," he said. "Please try to get some sleep; I'll see you in the morning."

Amelia said nothing further, as Dawson closed the door behind him.

It is an unsettling thought when a child falls to sleep at night not knowing the well-being of their parents. Unfortunately for Amelia Black, this thought was a very real and very frightening thought.

BUMP. Went the night.

"What was that," thought Amelia. "Dawson?" she whispered.

No answer.

"...Dawson?"

THUMP. Went the night again.

The sound was getting closer and closer. It clearly was not Dawson as it would not have been proper for him. He was a gentleman's gentleman, after all.

Amelia was beginning to feel very anxious. A burglar? A murderer?! Perhaps even a ghastly monster, like the sort she would find in her enormous library of enchanted books.

The strange noises were getting closer. Out of nowhere a shining light came inexplicably through the walls of her bedroom and lit up the entire room. Amelia was terrified. The floating spiral of light got closer and closer and suddenly...

WHACK. With all the girl's might!

Amelia swatted the thing and extinguished the light instantly. However, this was no mere light, nor indeed your typical care-free firefly.

"Oi! Do you treat all house guests like that?!" a voice screamed from the floor.

III

STANDING before Amelia, at a delicate height of exactly two-and-a-half inches, was a shabbily dressed man with a dirty beard, smoking a pipe that was emanating a small purple glow. Amelia was in complete shock and struggled to find a response to the stranger's incredible presence.

"What's wrong, kid? Cat got your tongue?"

"Um... I... Uh... What are you?" asked the girl, hesitantly.

"Pardon me? I am not a 'What,' I am a 'Who,'" snapped the tiny stranger.

"I'm sorry, that was awfully rude of me, sir..."

"So was swatting me, but I'm willing to let that go..."

"...Sorry, you just frightened me. What is your name?" she asked, feeling more settled.

"Sid."

"Well... Sid, pleased to meet you. My name is Amelia."

"Oh, I already know you, Ms Black. That's partly the reason I'm here."

"Really? What was the other reason?"

"Oh, you know, I like to fly around creepy mansions scaring the living daylights out of young, helpless little children."

The sarcasm was, however, lost on poor Amelia, who had been through enough as of late.

"...Yeah, so the reason I'm here..." Sid went on to explain.

"Are you a fairy?!" Amelia jumped in delight.

"NO!" Sid was annoyed by this, for he believed it to be common knowledge that it is offensive to his kind to be referred to as a fairy. "For your information, I am a pixie; a fairy is quite a different being altogether."

A silence awkwardly fell upon this unlikely encounter, which the girl dutifully broke, being the host to her mysterious guest.

"What's the difference between fairies and pixies, if you don't mind me asking, Mr Sid?" she asked, rather innocently.

"That doesn't matter," he said, with a frustrated sigh. "Look, back to the issue at hand, I've been sent to this uncouth realm to take you to an audience with the King of the Unseen Light."

"Why me?"

"Why not?" asked Sid, casually.

"But I can't. I live here," she explained. "And Dawson would be most worried about me."

"Bring him along. The King always says the more guests, the better."

"I just can't," she replied. The pixie knew by the tone of her voice there was nothing keeping her there other than some troubling anxiety.

"Oh, come on! Where's your sense of adventure?" asked Sid, cheerfully.

The pixie's question hit the poor girl hard. Oodles of memories of her loving and wonderful parents came flooding back into her head. It was as if a tiny light bulb magically appeared over her head and for the first time in a long time she felt as though there were someone out there, calling to her. Maybe it was the Unseen King the pixie spoke of, or maybe, just *maybe,* it was the longing for a real adventure that she had always dreamed of.

"Dawson, Dawson, come quickly!" shouted Amelia, as she came rushing into his chambers.

"Ms Black! What's going on? Did you have a bad dream?" Dawson sprang from his bed as if he was a solider standing to attention awaiting orders.

"No, Dawson, we're going on an adventure."

"An adventure, Ms? In the middle of the night? This is most unorthodox."

"Yes, Dawson. Mr Sid, the pixie, is taking us to the land of the Unseen King," she announced.

Dawson, being a practical man of sound and sensible judgement, was naturally sceptical of his young employer's fantastical travel plans. "Now, Ms Black, I understand you have been through a lot these past few months but it might be best to pass up on this 'Sid's request and try to get a good night's sleep."

"I'm awfully sorry, Dawson. That was terribly rude of me. Let me introduce Mr Sid..."

The faithful butler had become slightly curious about his young employer's actions, thinking the grieving child must have invented an imaginary friend as a natural response to the disappearance of her parents. He was even more perplexed, therefore, when he felt a tug on his bedclothes and heard a tiny voice, from an even tinier person, shout up at him:

"Oi, down here!"

"Goodness gracious!" exclaimed Dawson. Just like his young employer, he was deeply intrigued by the stranger standing before him. He attempted to pick Sid up, examining him like a mere insect instead of treating him like the tiny, proud person he was. That is, until Sid decided in a fit of rage that it was appropriate to bite Dawson's finger.

"Bloody humans," moaned Sid. "Always poking and prodding things they don't, nor will ever, understand."

"Dreadfully sorry, sir," said Dawson, in a genuinely apologetic tone.

"Enough of this apologetic trollop from the both of you, we must hurry quickly."

"How do we get to this 'Land of the Unseen King', Mr Sid?" asked Amelia.

"We take a trip through a desk drawer, take a left after the *mysterious* badger's hole, pass the fourth star on the left, then click our heels a couple of times in the best pair of shoes money can buy."

"Really?!" screamed Amelia, in utter delight.

"No, not really. That's just silly."

Dawson began to lose his patience with the ill-mannered pixie, which was not his usual conduct, and enquired firmly, "Well speak up man; some of us would rather just sleep on this cold, windy night."

"Well, Dawson, you've actually hit the beast firmly on the jaw."

"Excuse me?"

"Sleep! That's it. Well, sort of. There's a bit of hocus-pocus and spectacular mumbo-jumbo thrown in too," explained Sid. "You know, magic!"

"Magic?" asked Dawson, incredulously.

"Uh, yeah, normally I'm not very good at this," explained Sid, frantically searching his grimy pockets for something he appeared to have lost in transition. "We pixies aren't exactly known for being the most magically talented beings in the Unseen Universe." Then the spritely, miniature being brought out a crumpled piece of paper, dusted it off and smiled in delight, "Ah, here it is! Okay, let's give this a try, it should work..."

"And if it doesn't?" asked Dawson.

"We might end up in some alternative dimension or something like that," said Sid, casually. "Anyone ever told you you worry too much, Dawson?"

"Only for the well-being of my employer, sir," said Dawson, sternly.

"Oh, Dawson, do calm down please," said Amelia. "It'll be fine. Mr Sid knows what he's doing. Don't you, Mr Sid?"

"'Course I do; I'm no foolish conjurer of tricks," he declared, boisterously. "I can't be. I don't have any grey hairs, for a start."

Amelia was not sure what the pixie meant, but she was excited nevertheless.

So a slightly over-eager Amelia and a slightly wary Dawson lay their heads down and cleared their heads, which was indeed easier said than done considering the extraordinary circumstances. As they began to nod off, Sid started to whisper the spell to start the magic:

"Sleeping through all things,

I dream on and on,

When the world appears unseen,

I still dream on and on..."

Amelia heard these words, repeating over and over, getting quieter and quieter while she was getting sleepier and sleepier, until suddenly she found herself waking up to the most breathtaking sight imaginable.

IV

BEFORE Amelia and Dawson's very eyes lay a world of great beauty, like nothing they had ever seen before. Floating mountains, the sky steadily changing colour from blue to green to orange to yellow, giant swirling trees and lush beautiful valleys.

"The ever-changing sky might look pretty at first," mused Sid. "But after a while it does get bloody irritating."

The girl and her butler, however, took little notice of their guide's critical observations, as they admired the enchanted surroundings. The travelling pair's clothing had also drastically changed. Amelia was now wearing a beautiful – yet practical – dress flushed in various shades of her favourite colour, violet, and a pair of antique goggles were resting on her forehead. Dawson, now foregoing his nightwear, looked as refined and dapper as a gentleman's gentleman ought to for such an adventure. Suffice it to say, he was impressed with the results.

"What is this place?" asked Amelia in complete awe.

"It is what you choose it to be," explained Sid.

"I don't understand," said Amelia

"Everything before you, the trees, the rivers, the skies, the whole world including myself, is made from pure imagination," Sid clarified.

"That's impossible," Dawson proclaimed, with much scepticism despite the miraculous mode of transportation he and his young employer had just experienced.

"Improbable, maybe. But impossible, Dawson? No such thing."

"Excuse me, Mr Sid, but do you mean to say that everything here is a figment of my imagination?" asked Amelia.

"*Your* imagination? Steady on, there, Ms Black," said Sid, in a condescending tone. "This whole imaginarium, this whole *world,* was created and sustained through the power of one man. At least we think he's a man... there's a bit of debate about that one. Amelia Black. Julius Dawson. Welcome to the Light of the Unseen Universe."

Amelia's attention began to wander as she immersed herself in the Light. In the dale below there were strange creatures like nothing she had seen in any measly encyclopædia. Some with coloured fur and some who preferred to be called 'sir'. A few with hats and monocles, others who just liked to sit on the lush grass and read the weekly chronicle. You might think it all sounds quite plausible, yet these creatures measured up to ten feet tall, with ghastly teeth larger than a child's hand.

"What are they?" asked Amelia.

"Oh, they're Wolpertingers. Peaceful folk, despite their beastly appearance," said Sid. "Don't concern yourself too much with them; we have to keep moving. The palace is just beyond Fáfnir Forest."

Fáfnir Forest was a strange place, like no forest Amelia or her faithful butler had ever come across. The first thing she noticed upon entering this enchanted terrain was not the trees, so tall that they seemed not to have an end, nor the walking, living, breathing people made from what appeared to be sandalwood. No, the first thing Amelia noticed was a beautiful glow illuminating the entire forest, like floating fairy lights on a Christmas tree.

"Are they Fair... I mean, Pixies?" she asked.

"Good of you to remember the correct term, Ms Black," said Sid firmly. "This is where my kind have lived for longer than time itself, under the watchful eye of our King beyond the forest. Here we are free to do what we please, living amongst the Sandalwoods in harmony. Well, mostly."

"Mostly?" asked Dawson.

"Uh, yeah, you know how it is – a man is in his local tree, the locally-brewed dust is being knocked back, one thing leads to another... I don't think we should talk about this in front of the girl, Dawson," said Sid.

The pixies, Sid's kind, were thought to be a wild yet considerate bunch amongst the other inhabitants of the forest. The Sandalwoods, on the other hand, were thought to be a wise breed and often known to impart rare wisdom to anyone kind enough to ask.

Amelia was spellbound by the festival-like atmosphere of her new surroundings. She instantly fell in love with every aspect of the so earthly sounds and enchanting activities. Young Sandalwoods playing artlessly in the river, pixies singing merrily, old oaks musing by the corner.

Whilst in the vicinity, Sid felt obliged to introduce Dawson to some of the finer drinks of the Fáfnir Forest, his being a man of refined taste, after all. While they were doing such boring, grown-up things, Amelia decided to wander around the forest a bit; curiouser and curiouser, one might say.

Idling, she contemplated introducing herself to the young tree-folk who were playing in the sparkling clear river, until she was called over by a weak, gravelly voice, "You there..."

Amelia turned to see an old tree pointing at her. "Me, sir?" she asked.

"Yes, child. What is your name?"

"Amelia," she said, hesitantly. "Amelia Black."

"Are you afraid of the Dark, Amelia Black?" asked the earthly being, mysteriously.

"No, I don't suppose I am," she said, not really understanding the nature of the question.

"You will be," it said.

Amelia felt a slight chill run through her body, but just then she heard the comforting call of Dawson telling her it was time to move on before he indulged in too much gumberry juice. She leeched onto Dawson's hand, once again feeling safe and secure. She looked back to see the strange forest being walk slowly away in the opposite direction. It would be the first and last time the girl would ever encounter the mysterious tree, but the words would resonate for long after.

The trio moved on through the remainder of Fáfnir Forest, attracting little attention from the natives. The residents of the forest had become accustomed to seeing strangers passing through on the way to the palace and as long as they did not bother them, they were kind enough to return the favour.

What felt like hours later, they finally emerged from the forest and could see the magnificent palace far off in the distance. It was a spectacular structure consisting of five glass towers: four placed at each corner of the grounds, all converging into a spiralling vortex, with a fifth tower at the centre of the keep, at least a mile higher than the others. Like many of the structures and surroundings in this would so far, it emitted the most strikingly beautiful colours.

"Finally," Sid sighed with relief.

"That's the most beautiful palace I have ever seen," gasped Amelia.

"*Un*-seen," said Sid, playfully correcting the young explorer.

The trio continued on the road ahead, until suddenly a dark cloud gathered over them and from nowhere they heard a bloodcurdling scream, like the sound of a person in the most unimaginably frightening pain.

"No... no... it can't be... not here... not now! We were so close!" cried Sid. "Quick, hide in that ditch and don't dare come out!"

"What is it, Sid?" shouted Dawson.

"It's Ulana!"

"Who? What?!"

"Imagine a demon crossed with the body of a bird, and then multiply the size by ten, and you only get half the picture."

What Sid said about Ulana was true. At least thirty feet tall, giant claws big enough to pick up a full-grown man, horrid bat-like wings, piercing green eyes and chilling dead grey skin. Sid, the brave soul, tried to distract it for as long as possible, hoping it would give up this deathly pursuit, but that only made the beast angrier.

"GIVE ME THE GIRL!" screamed Ulana with a terrifying snarl.

"Never!" Sid declared. Weaving in and out of the beast's grasp, he was not getting anywhere. Amelia was beginning to fear for her guide's life. The spirited pixie managed to strike the gruesome beast right in the eye, but it did little to stop Ulana's pursuit of the girl.

"We should do something, Dawson," said Amelia, decisively.

"I don't think we're quite equipped to tackle hideous, giant beasts, Ms."

Now, Dawson was hardly one to be considered a coward, but he did have a lot of common sense when it came to life-threatening situations. Amelia was scared in a way she never thought possible. Her only wish right now was to save the pixie she considered a friend. Remarkably, upon Amelia having these thoughts, Sid was magically transported to cover with the girl and her butler.

"What just happened?" asked Sid, mystified.

"I don't know... we thought you did that."

"I'm capable of many things, but the ability to vanish and appear hundreds of metres away isn't one of them."

"Are we safe?" asked Dawson.

"No, Ulana is a cold-blooded predator, it will pick up our scent quickly. We must make a run for it."

The travelling trio looked beyond the ditch. The palace was too far away to make it before Ulana picked them up. Amelia's thoughts once again began to wander.

"If only we had a cage, or something to hold it," she pondered.

"Where do you suppose we would get one of those? Wait, I'll just check my pockets... Oh, what a surprise, nothing there" said Sid, sarcastically. His tolerance of the young girl was beginning to thin, under the immense pressure of the situation.

But strangely, upon Amelia's words, the most amazing thing had happened. A giant cage, not too dissimilar to a bird cage, locked itself around Ulana.

"What the..." Sid was starting to catch on to what might be happening. "Quick," he said, "let's make a run for it!"

They made a dash for the palace. Amelia started to fall behind and tripped on a rock in the open space. Dawson ran back furiously and threw the girl over his shoulder, carrying Amelia the rest of the way as they entered the palace of the Unseen King. The trio were safe, for now.

V

AS Amelia and her modest band entered The Great Hall of The Unseen Light – also known to most dwellers of the palace as, Magisterius Hall – she was left feeling numb, shaken and overwhelmed from the attack of that ghastly, demonic beast, Ulana.

Dawson held her like a father, as she began to burst into tears. "There, there, Ms. It's over now. We're safe," said Dawson. "What in the heavens was that?" He demanded, turning his attention to Sid.

"That, Dawson, was perhaps the most horrid being from the darkest, most twisted realm of the Unseen Universe," said Sid. "The Dark..."

"But I thought this was supposed to be a land of peace and enchantment?" said Dawson

"You can't have the Light without the Dark, Dawson. It's as constant in the universe as good and evil, right and wrong, cats and dogs, pixies and... fairies."

At this moment, Sid was interrupted by Sullivan, the Unseen King's royal advisor and scholar in residence. He was an exceptionally tall man with long, grey hair and a wild-looking beard that was nearly the length of young Amelia herself. "Mr Sid, we saw the beast. Are you all alright?" he asked.

"We are, no thanks to your guards," snapped Sid.

"We had no time. The King could not have foreseen that Ulana would know of the girl's presence. This complicates matters," he explained.

Overhearing this new piece of information, Amelia wiped her tears, composed herself and approached Sullivan. "Excuse me, sir, I would like to know: how does my being here complicate matters?" she asked.

"Amelia Black, what a pleasure it is finally to have you in our presence. You are our most honoured guest," said Sullivan, trying to change the subject.

"You didn't answer my question. What could I possibly have done to offend that monster?"

"Well, to be honest, my dear, these aren't questions I should be answering. I think we should move you into the Chamber of Thoughts; the King is expecting you." At this point, two stumpy, mechanical, copper-plated creations appeared from two side-doors within the magnificent entry. "Boris, Towser, please escort Ms Black to the Chamber of Thoughts."

"Right, boss," said Boris.

"No problem, boss," said Towser.

"Just don't get lost this time. If I have to plunge myself into the Abyss again and save your artificial souls, you will be sweeping up unicorn droppings for the next hundred years," said Sullivan, breaking from the manner with which he conducted himself with Amelia.

"Right, boss," said Boris, once again.

"No problem, boss," Towser repeated.

Sullivan mumbled, infuriated. In an instant, from around another bewildering corner of this even more bewildering structure, appeared a peculiar humanlike soul with a wrinkled face and short, curly, brown hair, who was dressed in brown clothing.

"MRSULLIVAN!" it shouted.

"Yes, Joost," replied Sullivan, "what is it?"

"WENEEDYOUINTHELIBRARYURGENTLYSIR. URGENTBUSINESS. THEBOOKWORMSAREATITAGAIN..."

"Again?" the old man thought out loud. "May the Light save us. My dear, I'm afraid I must depart but we'll get better acquainted soon, I'm sure." And so, Sullivan scuttled down the very, very, very long hallway in the opposite direction, fading gradually into the distance.

"He seems nice," said Amelia.

"Nice?" replied Sid. "Crazy old lunatic, more like..."

Amelia, Sid and Dawson were now under the guidance of the two mechanical robots. As they were being escorted down the hallway, it was the first chance Amelia had had to really marvel at the vastness of the castle.

The palace itself was incredibly old; older than Amelia could ever possibly comprehend. There were tall pillars, shining as bright as the sun. An endless mirror could be seen, covering the highest ceilings. Servants, scholars, knights and wisemen were rushing in and out of rooms and hallways.

While walking down the long hallway she could hear whispers, sounds of children playing and happy laughter. "Where are all these sounds coming from?" she asked.

"It's the sound of billions of dreams from billions of children currently sleeping in the Seen Universe," said Boris.

"Well said, Boris," concurred Towser.

"I thought so myself, Towser," replied Boris.

Sid was starting to see why Sullivan's patience would be tested on a daily basis in the presence of this duo.

"Why do the dreams of children matter to this place?" asked the girl.

"Beats us; we're just robots..." said Boris.

Before Amelia could ask anymore questions the party had arrived at a colossal gateway, with an incredibly complex design spiralling around an intriguing looking symbol.

"Alright, in you go, the King is waiting."

"Thank you, for your assistance," Amelia said, graciously.

As Amelia, Dawson and Sid attempted to walk through the door, Boris and Towser stopped them once more. "Only the girl may go in; the butler and the fairy must wait outside."

"The *what?*" asked Sid. From the expression on Sid's tiny face, Dawson could see where the conversation was going.

"...Fairy?" said Boris innocently.

This, as you could guess by now, did not sit well with Sid, and he decided it would be appropriate to throw a spear into the mechanised eye of Boris. Only then was the matter officially closed.

"Was it something I said?" the robot asked Towser, while walking away.

Amelia did as requested, understandably intimidated by the whole affair. She had never had the pleasure of meeting a king before, let alone a king of a magical world.

VI

WHEN Amelia walked into the Chamber of Thoughts, she was startled to find she was not in a room at all. Instead, she found herself in a beautiful garden, with feathery, white snow falling from a pale blue sky. She wondered, rather curiously it must be said, where the snow was coming from. There were no clouds in the sky, nor was it even remotely cold.

Her surroundings were minimal. All she could see upon a blinding white blanket was an unusual-looking tree and a tall, dark figure standing underneath.

"Welcome, Amelia Black," the mysterious figure came into the light.

Amelia saw he was a relatively old man, draped in black robes. He was unlike any kind of royalty she had seen in her countless fairytale books back home, with no distinctive crown or any real majestic jewellery apart from a strange and mysterious amulet he wore on a chain around his neck.

"My name is Loren. The Last King of the Unseen Light."

"It's an honour to meet you, your majesty," said Amelia.

"The honour is truly mine, child."

"I don't understand..."

"I'm sure you have many questions. I will do everything in my power to answer them."

"I must know, your majesty, why I am here?"

The King was evasive and shifted from the girl's question. "I'm sure the encounter with Ulana is still fresh in your mind, yes?" he asked. "Did you stop to wonder how your friend, the pixie, was able to transport himself to your hiding spot within seconds? And why a cage magically appeared to trap the beast long enough so that you and your friends could safely reach the palace?"

"Yes, I must say I did..."

"Look within."

"I... I still don't understand," said Amelia, starting to sound just as dazed as she was confused.

"Hold out your hand..." said Loren. "Now close your eyes and envisage something, anything." Amelia did as she was told. The girl concentrated with all her might and nothing happened. "You're trying too hard. Free your mind." Amelia tried again, and it was as if a consoling silence had settled upon the land. Suddenly, an enchanting rose appeared, floating over the palm of her hand. "Now, open your eyes."

The girl was amazed, looking curiously at the conjured object. She reached out and grabbed hold of the rose. "Is this real?" she asked.

"It's as real as you want it to be. Do not limit yourself with simple human reasoning," he explained. "Let your mind run free. This is just a rose, but you can make it so much more."

Amelia closed her eyes again as the rose started to levitate in mid-air. This time the flower started to transform: the stem began to multiply and intertwine and branch off, and within a matter of seconds the simple, elegant flower had altered into a magical archway with a thousand roses converging towards each other.

"This is amazing," said Amelia, in complete awe.

"Quite." The tone of Loren's voice had changed drastically. It was much more solemn and reflecting than it was initially with the girl. Amelia noticed this.

"You didn't bring me here just to show me this, did you?" she asked.

"I regret, Amelia, that I did not. You see, my time in this universe is slowly drawing to an end. As you may have noticed from my title, I am the last of my kind."

Amelia was not exactly sure what he meant by this, but she could tell that it deeply troubled and saddened Loren.

VII

"WHAT do you mean?" asked Amelia. At this point, Loren took her hand and suddenly the girl could see, hear and feel all of the King's memories. Before her eyes lay a desolate landscape, an absolute contrast to the lush, vivid world she was just in. She could hear Loren's voice echoing in the distance.

"Long ago, my people travelled the universe," he explained. "Through all dimensions of time and space, encountering all kinds of life, we eventually arrived in this world. It was a barren land, a canvas begging to be painted on. And so we discovered that with our unique powers we were able to craft a world in our own vision and create the magical creatures that would populate it. It was a peaceful time. We had finally found our place in the universe and had a new responsibility to a place we called home."

Amelia was able to see the beginnings, the magical construction of Fáfnir Forest, the inspiring assembly of the amazing palace. She even got a glimpse at the other wonders this miraculous world had to offer.

"Unfortunately, this age of peace and prosperity was not to last." A gasp of unspeakable fires, pain, horror and cold visions of death filled Amelia's head. It was too much to bear for a child's mind; she screeched as if she was there herself.

"Why are you showing me this?!" she cried. "Stop! Please, stop!" Loren granted the girl's request and broke off the visions. "I'm sorry, Amelia. I did not mean to cause you any distress."

Amelia was panting heavily, pale in the face, shaking from what she had just witnessed. "What... what was that?"

"That's when the Dark descended."

"The Dark?" asked Amelia. She remembered what the cryptic old tree had said to her in the Forest earlier. "What is it?"

"Over time, some of my kind became too greedy with their power, forgot their responsibility to the world they created and turned from creators into conquerors. The land was ravaged. The peaceful beings were turned into slaves. New, darker, killer beings were soon created to fight in an endless war. We had to act. It was a living nightmare. The Unseen Universe was torn, literally, in two. Millions of lives lost and regrettably only a handful survived."

"What does this have to do with me? I'm just a girl, a... a... nobody."

"Through a series of strange events, this now has everything to do with you." He held out his hand once again, "I promise, this will not hurt."

This time, Amelia saw two people, trapping themselves, in a secluded chamber. They appeared similar in stature and appearance to Loren, a man and a woman performing, what she could only imagine was a magic spell. It was to her astonishment she heard them recite something very familiar:

"Sleeping through all things,

I dream on and on,

When the world appears to be seen,

I still dream on and on..."

Then with a thunderous flash of white light, they disappeared! "Where did they go?" she asked.

"They fled this world, disillusioned by the tragedy of war brought upon their home." Loren put his hand on the tree in a somewhat reflective manner and spoke softly to himself, "in truth, I can't say I blame them." He turned back to the girl with a more commanding presence, like a preacher on a mount, "like several others, they escaped to various dimensions untouched by this pain and suffering. One dimension you might even call home."

"That doesn't make sense," said Amelia, with a measure of good confidence in her reasoning. "Surely I would have read about these amazing people capable of such amazing powers."

"Perhaps, but upon arriving in the Seen Universe they realised their abilities were rendered useless. Accepting their situation, knowing they could never go back, they settled to raise a family, happily content to forget the condemned world they left behind. For generations their tree grew, filled with love, truth, success and wealth. Two worlds linked by one family. Black."

VIII

AMELIA was besieged by the latest revelations. So undeniably mystified, the girl was hardly sure what to believe anymore; what was real or what was a dream.

"So... I'm one of you, I'm... well... whatever you are?" she asked.

A reflective glance shot across Loren's face. He even released a relaxed smile to calm the girl's nerves. "No, you are very much human, think of yourself as a distant cousin of my race. You shall always be Amelia Black from the Seen Universe, but in here you possess a rare power that could change the course of history in the blink of an eye. A power Ulana would use for its own monstrous gain."

"Well can't we just tell him... her... whatever it is, that I mean no harm? My mother and father taught me never to hurt animals, if Ulana even is an animal..." she replied.

Loren's expression once again turned stern. "Not yet," he said.

"What do you mean, not yet?"

"Amelia, this is very important." Loren began to grow tired of the confused girl's hysterics. "Your immense power is something far greater than mine. Ulana wished to lure you here in order to seize your power and use it to destroy all that is good. Fáfnir, this palace, the inhabitants, everything would be covered in darkness."

"I'm harmless. I am not some evil, horrible grown-up! This has nothing to do with me!" she screamed.

The tears descended frantically down her colourless face, the sky began to darken once more and suddenly an immense explosion, full of magical mist and colour erupted violently within the chamber. All that was, was now destroyed.

The dust eventually settled to reveal the Chamber to be nothing more than a plain white room, with Amelia and Loren standing in the middle.

The King walked over to a door, barely noticeable to the sharpest of eyes. "I think that's enough revelations for one day. Please let us reconvene in The Amalricus Room. Dinner will be served shortly; your friends are waiting," he said delicately, while escorting Amelia to the exit.

IX

THE Amalricus Room was as wondrous as its title suggests. A striking, never-ending space, decorated with some of the most inspiring pieces of art found in the Seen and Unseen Universes. Although Amelia was a well-educated and cultured sort, she was, perhaps, too young to know where the majority of the art may have hailed from, but marvelled nonetheless.

There were towers of bookshelves, holding the works of every author ever to live, located between each archway. She couldn't wait to read all of them. The entire room was lit up by the most enchanting fairy lights floating throughout the vast space, similar to the stars Amelia would see through her father's telescope on the coldest of winter nights.

The girl's interest peaked as she plucked one of the lights in mid-air, treasuring it in her hand. Its glow began to dim to reveal an unusual diamond in the shape of a lantern. She then, proudly, threw the strange tiny object back into the air and was in awe as it zipped off, like a shooting star, down the never-ending room.

She approached the table situated at the centre of the hall beneath a beautiful stained-glass dome, to find Dawson and Sid waiting anxiously for her return.

"Ms Black, thank goodness, are you alright?" asked Dawson, giving his young employer a comforting hug, which he seemed to need more than our dear heroine.

"She's perfectly fine, Dawson," replied Loren

"I can speak for myself thank you, your *majesty*," Amelia interrupted. She then turned to Dawson, smiling, thankful to be reunited with her faithful butler and lifelong friend. She gave him a much needed, rather comforting hug.

"Um... I'm here too!" cried Sid. Amelia smiled; of course she had not forgotten her mindboggling Pixie guide.

"Please do sit down, it's time for tea," said Loren gently. They politely did what was requested of them. However, Dawson was slightly perplexed as to why there were only four seats for such a large table, which stretched at least one hundred feet. Even the main dining table in Amelia's family mansion was not this long and, lest we forget, that was fit or a king or indeed a queen.

"This is slightly ostentatious, if you don't mind me saying, sir?' said Dawson, trying not to offend his prestigious host.

"Hmm... perhaps it is, Dawson. Amelia, could you adjust the dimensions for us, please?" said Loren.

Dawson was offended that the King asked the girl when he, surely in his duties as the host, should have offered to do it himself or at least have his own help provide the service.

Amelia lightly closed her eyes and within seconds, as if the table sprung to life, it retracted down to a sensible size, surely no bigger than a formal dining table found in most households in the Seen world.

However, the young girl went one further, as wonderful, glorious, scrumptious foods and desserts started to appear on the table and carts surrounding the guests. A lip-

59

smacking turkey dinner, with all the trimmings, similar to the kind Dawson would cook the Blacks at Christmas. Actually, in Amelia's mind it *was* the exact recipe the kindly butler used long ago.

"What... no baby carrots drenched in honey, just like mummy use to make?" replied Sid. Amelia was kind enough to oblige her Pixie friend.

"Ho-ho-ho!" Sid screamed in delight. However, much to his dismay, when he dived into the succulent carrots he inevitably found that the carrots in question were, in fact, nothing like his mother's own. How young Amelia was supposed to know this, should have dawned upon our fair pixie. Unfortunately it did not, and Sid was left feeling underwhelmed by the results.

"This is madness!" Dawson proclaimed. "What have you done to her?" he yelled at the King.

"Nothing that would bring her to any harm, let me assure you," the King calmly replied.

"It's okay Dawson," said Amelia, "I don't really know what to make of all this, but it seems my ancestors came from this wondrous place and I have inherited this rather peculiar power," the girl explained. Her entire face lit up with excitement, like a child on Christmas morning, "it's really amazing, isn't it?"

Dawson was unconvinced, and his emotions remained stern. He brought out his golden pocket watch, gazed sparingly at the time, and thought it was best to end this nonsense, for Amelia's sake.

"Ms Black, I do believe it's time we departed this world and returned to our own," he said.

"What? But, no, Dawson, we can't! There's so much more to explore! I don't want to go!" she said.

Dawson stood up, grabbed Amelia by the hand and started to walk out of The Amalricus Room. The girl tried to fidget away from her guardian but he held her firm.

"Your majesty, thank you for your hospitality but we must be going," said Dawson.

"The pleasure was all mine, Dawson, you are both welcome back any time..." said Loren, gracefully. "Of course, if you go now, the girl won't find out where her delightful parents are being held..." Amelia and Dawson both froze, as a tidal wave of emotions rose instantly from their stomachs.

"What did you just say?" said Dawson.

X

"WHERE are they?" asked Dawson.

"Oh, you're going home, I wouldn't want you to worry..." said Loren, candidly.

The butler angrily grabbed the King, by his robes, pinning him up against the wall. Suddenly one hundred guards, wearing black and gold armour, magically appeared out of nowhere and surrounded the butler. Of course, logic would dictate if one could conjure anything, one would never need to actually employ standard guardsman. Loren eased and confessed this revelation to Amelia and Dawson.

"The girl's parents are currently being held within Ulana's chilling fortress, beyond the cruel labyrinth, at the centre of the Malus Mountains."

"We have to go!" cried Amelia, hysterically. "Right now!"

"That's just what Ulana wants you to do, my child," explained Loren

"I don't care, this is my mother and father, we have to save them." A look of idle desperation fell over the poor girl, "I have to save them."

"With all due respect, Amelia," interjected the King of the Unseen Light, "although you are capable of inflicting great power on your enemy, realise this: you are young and you can be easily swayed."

"I know the difference between right and wrong, your *majesty*," retorted Amelia.

"There's more to this than knowing the difference between right and wrong, Amelia. The beast is more powerful than you can imagine."

"...He means that literally, y'know..." said Sid.

Loren chose to ignore the pixie, as this was hardly the time for his bone-headed humour, he thought. "It's far too dangerous. I hope you can understand that. The fate of this realm is at stake. You are its last hope. All that has happened has happened before, and it could all happen again."

Amelia looked forlorn. Pale and dejected, it was neither the place nor the situation for a girl her age to be in. She held onto Dawson's hand and her head fell like a fallen champion, giving up. Perhaps it was time to go home. She yearned to wake up from this dream until her imagination conjured up something she had not had the courage to look at in a very long time: the Black family portrait – the only one of its kind.

Painted by one of the greatest classical artists of the time, Clément Peter Schubert, there sat her ever-loving parents, Aoibhinn and Antoine Black.

Humble and elegant, the pair of them, their sincere joy was unquestioned by the sight of baby Amelia sitting peacefully on Aoibhinn's knee. Barely a few weeks old but still as bright-eyed and radiant as the happiness she bestowed on her mother and father. Amelia had seen this painting what felt like a million times, but for the first time since meeting all these magical beings, and visiting this lush and prosperous world, it felt as though she was truly reminded where she had come from.

Wiping away the tears, Amelia let go of Dawson's hand, took a deep sigh, and let the anxiety fade away. She turned to face the Unseen King, this time putting her stubborn, brat-like attitude to one side.

"I hope you can understand this, I can't live without my parents. I lost them once, and don't want to lose them again. If you believe I'm 'the last hope' for this world then I need to do this, please don't stand in my way."

Loren might have been what some may call a stubborn ruler, but he was not an unfair one. "If that is what you wish," replied the King. "Provided you are able to find the Malus Mountains, of course..."

Sid, though loyal as he was to the King, had had enough of Loren's disdainful retorts. "I'll take her," he said. "I've been through the Dark once or twice. Always thought living was overrated these days..."

As before, Amelia was somewhat bewildered by Sid's cynicism but smiled nevertheless at her delightfully minuscule friend's courage.

"So be it," said the King, as he made a lonely exit down the seemingly endless hall. "You leave in two days, Amelia," he added. "I suggest you use the time to familiarise yourself with the realm and organise your companions. Dangerous times lie ahead." Suddenly a ruby coloured door magically appeared from nothing, and Loren had vanished into solitude, once more.

XI

FOR the next two days, Amelia and Dawson underwent rigorous preparation for the journey ahead.

To begin, the girl was given a series of exercises to help broaden her mind, which would allow her to expand her powers further. This involved conjuring simple objects from her new found power of imagination. Straightforward household items like a vase, a knife, a fork, an apple, a pear, even a tangerine. Yet strangely, she never could quite master the kitchen sink.

Afterwards, just like in the Chamber of Thoughts days earlier, she went about taking these objects and manipulating them to her own advantage.

Under the attentive guidance of the King's personal aide, Sullivan, the highly educated scholar in the science and art of dark imagination, she studied rigorously. The beasts and the perils and the dangers and the strangers they are likely to come across once they cross over into the Dark.

"What's this, Mr. Sullivan?" asked Amelia, wide-eyed and curious as always. Her gaze was transfixed on an image of a hunchbacked creature with its entire body engulfed in a black cloak.

"Oh, this? Yes! This!" he yelled in great delight. "This wretched, horrid individual is simply known as The Mute," explained Sullivan.

"So she's only horrible because she doesn't speak?" asked Amelia. "Doesn't really seem fair to bully a person because they don't speak, least that's what I've always been taught. They might just be shy!"

Sullivan was pleasantly surprised by the girl's well-natured manner, even though it was grossly misplaced and a little naive, he thought. "Quite so, my dear, but it is referred to as The Mute because it's looking for a voice."

"A voice?" she asked, curiously.

"Yes, a voice. In a drop of water, it yearns for a voice. Not to speak but to hold. It yearns for a voice."

"Sounds unsettlingly poetic," said Dawson.

"Indeed, though is there anything poetic in this 'thing' ripping your voice box from your throat and swallowing it for its own gain?"

"Hmm, I suppose not," the butler conceded.

"I wouldn't worry about The Mute too much; chances are you aren't going to find one en route to the Malus Mountains... I think."

Amelia and Dawson gave a glancing look at each other, suggesting they were not entirely convinced.

Moving swiftly on, Sullivan presented the next slide from his flamboyant projector, not too dissimilar from the type found in the local picture houses in Amelia's world.

"These people, on the other hand, are scattered throughout the region, particularly in the elusive Forgotten Forest. Disconcerting folk simply known as..." he paused for needlessly dramatic effect, lowering his voice, "The Watchers."

"What do they do?" asked Amelia.

"Unspeakable things, Ms Black! Horrible things! Things you wouldn't even wish on your worst enemy!" he exclaimed, hysterically.

"Well speak up man, what do they do?" demanded Dawson.

"They... *watch* you, Dawson," whispered Sullivan, nervously.

"And then what?"

"Nothing, they just keep watching you!" cried Sullivan.

"...That's it? They just keep watching us? Although it's incredibly ill-mannered, it's not exceedingly scary, if you don't mind my saying, sir."

The overly eccentric scholar of all that is good and evil leapt up on to the table and started poking the fair butler in the chest.

"You just don't get it, man! Imagine walking through a wild endless forest, all alone, with nothing more than dozens of those silhouettes just staring at you! It's made even the bravest of minds crumble into dust." Sullivan calmed himself down, and lowered the tone of his voice, as if he was telling a haunting story around a campfire. "Their horrific, mystifying hold over their victims will only grow, the more you are afraid."

Dawson's warranted cynicism sobered into a tense anxiety. Little did he and Amelia know this would not be the last they would hear about the terrifying fiends known as The Watchers.

Later that night, after Amelia was safe and secure in her elaborate bed chambers, Sullivan found Dawson gazing into the breathtaking sky full of wondrous mystery and enchantment. "Something troubling you, sir?" asked the scholar.

"Just this world. This castle. Your king. It's a lot to take in," said Dawson, solemnly. "I can see it as clear as daylight, touch it, feel it, smell it. I know the stumbles and falls and the terrifying monster I saw out there was all so real, yet here I sit still waiting to wake up."

"I realise how overwhelming this all might seem, Julius," said Sullivan.

"Ha, you called me Julius. I haven't been called that in a long time..." said Dawson, trying to shift the subject. Sullivan was not willing to humour him.

"Perhaps you were already at peace with the mysterious disappearance of the girl's mother and father? Reopening old wounds is never an easy thing. I may seem like an eccentric old fool, but..." he paused, realising he was merely caught up in the moment, "...never mind. My point is, as vague as it may seem, trust in the King..."

"That's the problem. I can't blindly follow a king I have little trust in, or commit to the salvation of a world I have even less stake in," said Dawson. "It... unsettles me. He unsettles me."

Sullivan gave a faint smile, and once more the pair gazed up at the stars above. "So, my friend, why are you here?" asked Sullivan.

"There's a little girl asleep in the next room and I made a promise to myself she would be protected at all costs," said the butler.

"Then, may I ask, what's in it for you?"

"Another chance to have some purpose in life. Whatever happens, the girl is the only family I have left and as long as she wishes to remain here, so will I."

Sullivan smiled again, "You know, there's this timeless rule of the universe that those who refuse to believe in magic will never find it," he said. "Thankfully for us, little Amelia has already found it. And someday Julius, you will too."

Dawson was not sure what the old man meant, but was too tired to question his strange ramblings.

"Now go, get some sleep, we have a long journey ahead of us tomorrow..."

XII

ON the morning of their departure, Loren treated the intrepid crew to a heroes' breakfast in The Amalricus Room, full of scrumptious delights, invigorating beverages and fine delicacies exclusive to the region. Including, fair reader, I jest you not, triple, no, quadruple helpings of Sid's Pixitrifle, a famous family recipe.

"The special ingredient is a hint of Vertly Leaves, mashed in with the Miaberries," explained Sid.

"Never would've pegged you as the culinary sort, Sid," said Dawson.

"Oh, so just because I can pick a fight with a monstrous beast a thousand times my own size and still manage to keep my limbs intact, I'm incapable of basic treehold skills? You trying to say that, Dawson? Well, are ya?!" cried Sid, in a rapturous rage.

"I was just pleasantly surprised, really. I would like the recipe sometime."

"Oh... okay."

Amelia, ignoring her fellow travellers' mild bickering, was beginning to feel a little weighed down by the enormity of the task ahead. She knew it would be days' travel to the Dark, never mind attempting to navigate their way through the dangers that lurked across the border.

"Well, the food was really yummy, your majesty, but I guess we really need to start travelling," said Amelia.

"Of course, my dear. *The Blanchard* awaits you and your companions in the courtyard," said Loren.

"Blanchard?" enquired Amelia. For perhaps the first time since her arrival, our dear heroine saw the King's eyes light up in flurry of excitement, like a child bursting to demonstrate his favourite toy in a show-and-tell day at school.

"Yes, Amelia, *The Blanchard*! Please, please, this way. You too, Dawson. This is simply too glorious to merely describe..."

The King ushered his honoured guests into the beautiful royal courtyard, where docked was the most magnificent airship ever conceived. A gigantic crystal-clear balloon, decorated with intricate patterns, filled with an assortment of multi-coloured gases to help elevate it into the air. At its base lay a control bay, powered by elaborate mechanisms and propulsion systems to help manoeuvre the ship over the beautiful landscapes this side of the world had to offer.

By the docking clamps, Boris and Towser were stocking up supplies in the control room, while Sid and Sullivan were plotting the best route on ancient maps from the palace's archives.

"Obviously we won't be able to fly the ship through the Dark, but using it to get to the border will easily cut over a week off our journey," explained Sullivan.

"Why can't we just fly it straight to the Malus Mountains?" Amelia enquired.

"Well, Amelia," explained Sid, "we're flying a gigantic balloon, powered by luminous multi-coloured gases, lit up like a Christmas tree, while on a rescue mission. It's hardly the most inconspicuous way to infiltrate the most evil, horrible, dark territory in the Unseen Universe, now, is it?"

"I guess, when you put it like that, it might not be the brightest of ideas..." Amelia conceded.

Meanwhile, Boris and Towser were conversing in a rather... philosophical manner.

"Have you been to the Dark before, Boris?" asked Towser.

"I have, Towser," said Boris.

"Really, Boris?" asked Towser.

"Indeed, Towser," replied Boris.

"What's it like, Boris?" enquired Towser.

"Dark," said Boris.

"No, no, *no!*" cried Sullivan, furiously. "You've never been to the Dark before, you mechanical nitwit! I just occasionally turn you off, and your program enters an empty void which just happens to be dark. Now get on the bloody ship!"

"No problem, boss," the robots responded, collectively. Sullivan, once again, released an uncontrollably frustrated sigh.

"So, Sully, why are we taking the dumb-bots?" asked Sid.

For a moment Sullivan struggled to think of an acceptable answer, but realised it made no difference as they were only robots and thus were completely emotionless. "I don't know... cannon fodder I guess. All they're really good for is carrying supplies. Once we've entered the Dark we're still days from the mountains."

"I see."

"So, when are we leaving, Mr Sullivan?" asked Amelia.

"When you give the order, my dear," said Sullivan. Amelia was slightly perplexed by the scholar's reply.

"Me?"

"This is your rescue mission, Amelia. We are only your crew. You possess an incredible power that we can only dream of. When it comes down to it, only you can save your parents; all we can offer is our guidance and help along the way."

Amelia did not quite know what to say; barely even a week ago she was a lonely little girl with no hope. Now, she found herself in command of a crew containing an overly eccentric scholar with an insanely long beard, an ill-tempered Pixie, two absent-minded robots and, of course, Dawson, no longer considered merely as a faithful butler but ultimately as a loyal friend to the end. Suddenly the world, Seen or Unseen, was not looking quite so bleak anymore.

"Amelia," said Loren. "I can't offer anything which may be of help to you on this voyage, but just remember, don't be afraid. No matter what you see or what you hear, please, don't be afraid. Your parents' lives may depend on it."

"Thank you, your majesty. I'll try." Then the intrepid explorer turned around to her crew in waiting and smiled. "Let's go!" she cried.

"That's more like it, Amelia!" cried Sid. "C'mon Dawson!"

Before boarding the magnificent ship Amelia grabbed Dawson's hand and gave him a huge hug. The butler smiled and his heart was warmer for it.

"We're going to save them, Ms Black," he said.

"Dawson?"

"Yes, Ms?"

"Can you please just call me Amelia from now on?"

"I can't make any promises, Ms Black, but I'll try... Amelia."

And so, with a pull of a lever here, a push of several buttons there, *The Blanchard* rose majestically into the sky, Amelia could see everything from King Loren's castle, in its entirety, to the constant glow from the beautiful and enchanted Fáfnir Forest, to the mysterious floating mountains, lush vibrant lands, and sacred monuments yet to be explored.

Many dangers await our courageous heroine, but no creature nor monster in all of creation could take away those few minutes of pure joy she felt from that first take off onboard *The Blanchard*. Her voyage may have started that fair night with a visit from Sid, but now Amelia's adventure had finally begun!

XIII

THE take-off was smooth and the crew was at ease for now. A comforting tranquility descended within the control bay of the marvelous *Blanchard*. However, Amelia could not help noticing Sullivan still bustling away at his maps and strangely complex compasses.

"Are you alright, Mr Sullivan?" asked the girl.

"Hmm? Oh yes, of course, Amelia. I'm fine. Thank you."

"You don't seem to be like anybody else from this place," observed Amelia. "Actually, I could almost swear you were from my world."

Sullivan stopped for a moment. Looked sternly into the eyes of the girl and then relaxed. "That's because I am," he replied.

"But why are you here?"

He removed his glasses and stared out at the mysterious world, with a faint, reminiscing smile. "I was once a professor at the Institute of Mythical Science and Alchemy," he said. "It was very prestigious. It was also very secretive. We kept to ourselves mainly, studying the truth behind all fairytales and legends that have dominated the imagination of our world for centuries. I firmly believed there was much more to it all than merely a master art of storytelling. It was harmless passion, really."

Amelia was amazed. She imagined spending all day analysing old fairytales and legends would have been so much fun. In a way it reminded our dear girl of her parents' profession exploring the hidden treasures scattered throughout her own realm.

"Wow!" she said. "And you were proved right! It must have been the greatest day of your life finding this place and meeting the King and all his subjects!" she gasped in excitement.

Sullivan smiled politely at the girl's innocence, as he reached for a glass of water. "Indeed, though the journey here was not an easy one," he explained.

"What happened?" she asked.

"It began like any other day, I suppose." The man's voice started to sound wry. "I was late that day. To the institute, I mean. Clara and I were up all night with the children."

"Children?" Amelia's curiosity suddenly peaked.

"Yes, Rebecca," he paused. "My little Becca and William." He started to sound overwhelmed. "Anyway, they were only one and two years old by this stage, they would often come into our bedroom late at night, my darling wife and I would rarely get any sleep. I wasn't much help, to be honest. I was often so fascinated by their vivid descriptions of their dreams and nightmares. Very bright children; even at that age, their intellect was remarkable. I had such high hopes for them."

"Had?" Amelia's concern grew larger.

"Yes. I was running late to the institute that morning, an important meeting of all the professors. We had been under a lot of pressure from local spiritual groups claiming we were practising with mumbo jumbo – black magic. We weren't too worried, admittedly. Empty threats, like all the rest, we thought."

"That's awful," gasped Amelia. "Some people are just... just... stupid!"

"I arrived at the institute, horrified to find the entire building surrounded by government guards," he continued. "One of our associates had betrayed us. I never found out who. All my friends, colleagues and assistants were rounded up, charged with committing blasphemy, and executed. I panicked. Ran for my life, hid everywhere, anywhere, even in neverwhere."

All the good man said was true; he had run for miles, hiding out in back alleys, in poor houses, even altering his appearance. It was not long until the authorities realised he was unaccounted for, making him a wanted man.

"I went back home to get Clara and the children, but I was too late. The house was shrouded in flames. They never made it out alive."

"Oh no..."

"So I just kept on running. I should've stayed and taken my punishment like a man."

"But you did nothing wrong," said Amelia.

"I failed to protect them." It must be pointed out, however, that Sullivan was not an emotionally troubled person and never got lost within himself in the telling of this story. He remained calm and collected throughout.

"I reached as far as the coast. Stole a boat and then set sail for wherever wasn't home."

He did not get very far. The sea and elements proved to be his undoing. His modest boat was ripped apart by the waves; all he could see before he blacked out was the cold, lonely moon glowing through the dispersing clouds, as he dropped deeper and deeper into an unknown abyss.

"And when I woke up I was here. The King had saved me from death. Couldn't believe my eyes, initially thought I had gone to heaven. In return for his selfless gesture, I dedicated the rest of my days to chronicling everything about this world," he said. "That was over 150 years ago."

For a split second a curious but reasonable thought came rushing into Amelia's head. "How do you know this isn't heaven?" she asked.

"They aren't here," he said, regretfully.

Suddenly *The Blanchard* started to bleep, sweep and creep. The mysterious border of the Dark was now fast approaching.

"Come now, the real work begins." The dear scholar exited into the control room. Amelia stayed behind and discreetly imagined another portrait out of thin air.

"Mr Sullivan?" she said.

"Yes?"

"This is for you!"

Unexpectedly, the dear scholar shed a small tear. Amelia had presented a child's rough painting of him and his family. The old man smiled gracefully.

"Thank you, Amelia," he said. "I shall cherish this forever."

Then, abruptly, something collided into the side of the airship.

CRASH.

BANG.

WALLOP.

Sparks flew from panels, steam leaked from everywhere while gears span out of control.

"What in the Dark was that?!" cried Sid.

"It's Ulana!" cried Dawson. The beast came back around to smash into the ship once again, this time breaching the hull. Its giant, horrid claw then proceeded to snatched Amelia from the control room.

Dawson tried to leap after her but was held back by Sullivan. "Don't do it, friend; you won't survive," he said. "Sid, you know what to do."

"Here we go again," he cried.

Just like last time, Sid flew brave and true towards the revolting beast, employing the same tactics as last time.

This time Ulana was ready for the valiant pixie, and swatted him away like a bothersome insect.

"YOU'RE MINE NOW, GIRL," snarled the beast.

"Amelia!" Sullivan shouted from the damaged ship. "Wish upon a shooting star!"

"WHAT?" said the monster. Rapidly out of nowhere a blinding light shone upon Ulana. Once again the girl had the upper hand, as a small, sparkling meteor struck the head of Ulana.

Amelia was falling, falling, falling. Gone.

"Amelia!" Dawson screamed once again, wanting to go after her, but his shipmates pulled him from harm.

"Dawson, stay focused! The ship is about to crash into The Forgotten Forest!" said Sullivan, commandingly. "Boris, Towser: try and cover those breaches in the hull!"

"Sure, boss," said Boris.

"No problem, boss," said Towser.

"Now isn't the time!" cried Sullivan. "Everybody brace yourselves."

The ship, however, did not pull through, as the sheer velocity of the descent ripped the entire control room in two. Sullivan, Sid and Dawson crashed into the depths of The Forgotten Forest, the unforgiving trees breaking their fall.

The robots, Boris and Towser, I fear were not so lucky, and went down on the other side of the barren wasteland in a ghastly explosive exit. But, you may ask, what of Amelia?

XIV

AMELIA crashed through the barren, lifeless trees of The Forgotten Forest, on to the muddy, unforgiving earth. The forest itself was vast, running the entire border between the Light and the Dark of the Unseen Realm.

With cuts and bruises showing all over her legs and arms, her dress reduced to tatters and her hair in a frightful state, all she wanted was for Dawson to come out of nowhere and help her home. Was Dawson even alive, she thought to herself? What about Sid? Or Sullivan? Or even Boris and Towser?

All of a sudden Amelia could hear whispers in her ear. Revolting and vile insults from children to adults, and it was all about her. Yet she could see nothing but darkness. Within seconds a spine-tingling voice came through the crowd of invisible. It was female. She was articulate and unsettlingly soft in her tone.

"Welcome," said the voice. "Welcome, Amelia Black."

"Who's there?" Amelia could hear the voice laughing.

"Aren't you just precious."

"Who are you?" asked Amelia.

"You know that prickling fear you sometimes get in the dead of night? That horrid nightmare, that feeling of complete and utter helplessness, that split second of despair, darkness and total isolation? I'm all of that, and more."

"You're... you're not Ulana," said Amelia. She began to tremble slightly.

"That tedious drone? No. I am its master, its creator. Its *goddess*."

"But that would mean you're like the King... I mean, like me... possess the same power," said Amelia.

"Same power? You delusional little brat, you can't begin to comprehend the power you wield," the voice snarled. "Silly little halfling. All of that human emotion inside of you. How disgusting. Just as weak and hideous as your mother. Such a poor, unfortunate soul."

"Shut up!" cried Amelia. "Go away!"

The voice continued to laugh inside the girl's head. "I am slightly disappointed, child," said the woman. "I was expecting you to get much farther than this quaint little forest before we met."

Amelia was disorientated as the voice seemed to come from all the areas around her.

"You know, Amelia, this isn't a total loss," it continued. "You can be my adorable little doll. I can dress you up and keep you on display in my palace. Oh, I have such sights to show you."

"No!" she screamed. "Get out of my head!" She began to cower in a little ball on the ground.

"Oh, I could leave, but then you'd be alone again, wouldn't you? And little Amelia Black doesn't like to be left alone, does she?" whispered the voice. "Look at yourself. A spoiled little rich girl, who is going to wither and die in this forest. Can't you see time is already starting to catch up with you?"

Suddenly Amelia's entire body began to age drastically. Her long, luxurious black hair decayed slowly into a ghostly white shadow of its former self. She could feel her body starting to turn unusually frail; she could barely stand on her own legs.

"Stop this, please," pleaded the girl, whose voice now sounded like that of an old, desperate, woman. But the vile voice continued to taunt her.

"Careful dear, if you have nothing valid to contribute to the conversation please don't speak at all..."

Next, Amelia's teeth started to fall out one by one, crumbling into dust with dark red blood gushing intensely from her mouth. The fear was becoming unbearable. She went into shock. The girl was barely able to catch a single breath.

"I suppose I could stop but I'm just having too much fun," mused the voice, in a deranged manner. "Oh, I wonder what will happen if I do this..."

Amelia began to melt slowly away, all of her body liquefied into a puddle of primordial ooze, resembling nothing one would even call a person anymore. This was the end, she thought.

Extraordinarily, in the blink of an eye, Amelia was fully restored to her true form. There was an unsettling silence.

"You didn't think I was going to let you go that easily?" whispered the voice. "I have bigger plans for you. Farewell, my darling, I'll be in touch."

Just like that, as if it was just some horrific nightmare, the grim presence of that mysterious voice left Amelia Black. But if it was not the demonic Ulana, then who was she?

With all her might the girl picked herself up and kept going, cautiously and fearfully. She had to. She knew she could not let her parents down.

XV

MEANWHILE, deep within the forest, Dawson, Sullivan and Sid clambered their way out of the shattered remains of the once magnificent airship.

"Well, that could have been worse," said Sid.

"How could that have possibly been any worse, Sid?" moaned Dawson.

"Well... we could be dead?" explained Sid.

Dawson did not seem to appreciate his companion's answer, while dusting the debris off his suit. "I knew it was a mistake agreeing to this, I should have taken Amelia home when I had the chance," he said.

"Hey, don't blame yourself, Dawson," said Sid, a bit more sympathetically than usual.

"I don't. I blame that insufferable King for putting ideas in her head."

"Quiet, the pair of you," interjected Sullivan. He had strangely kept his head to the ground, and then suddenly sprouted up to smell the cold dead air. "Can you hear that?"

"Hear what?" said Sid. "Darkness and death don't usually make a sound, just tend to smell like stink."

Sullivan paid little attention to Sid and started digging away at the debris.

"Sullivan, what *are* you doing?" asked Dawson.

"I'm searching for a compass, a map, even a flashlight. Something of genuine worth. We need to leave this part of the forest very quickly."

A disturbingly dark shadow fell upon the land. Sullivan froze.

"Now *this* complicates matters," said Sullivan

"It's them, isn't it?" said Sid, with a hint of fear in his voice.

"Don't move. Don't make a single sound," whispered the prudent scholar. "The Watchers loom..."

Indeed, creeping through the blackness, sinister silhouettes started to appear, doing nothing but anticipate the brave travellers' next move.

Dawson had never experienced dread like it. A disgustingly horrible, skin-crawling feeling. He felt his mind becoming entranced, losing all self-awareness.

"Dawson?"

The butler turned and froze at the sight before his tired eyes. "Mr and Mrs Black?"

Indeed, standing before him, just like the last time he had had the pleasure of seeing them, were Antoine and Aoibhinn Black.

"How could you let her die, Julius?" screamed Antoine.

"We trusted you with our most valued treasure, and you helped send her to her death," said Aoibhinn.

"No. This can't be. You're not real," said Dawson, the cold, sobering sweat dripping from his face.

"Murderer. Child murderer." They both whispered.

"I would give my life for Amelia, like she was my own daughter! You both know that," bawled Dawson, uncontrollably.

"Then give your life now," they said in unison.

Sullivan and Sid tried to snatch him from The Watchers' psychological hold. "Dammit, Dawson, listen to me. Whatever is going on inside your head, it's not real," said Sullivan. Sid even attempted to fly into Dawson's ear in a hopeless attempt to snap the butler from his twisted phantasmagory.

Sullivan collapsed to his knees. He could sense the sick, nefarious creatures taking over his own mind, and suddenly before his very eyes was a tragic ghost from his past. He took a deep breath.

"I know you're not real, be gone," he said.

"Is that any way to speak to your beloved wife?" said Clara.

"Not if she was really here."

"How could you let your own family burn in that fire? You black-hearted monster."

"Hush." Sullivan tried everything in his power to resist, but the presence of his departed wife grew stronger within his mind.

"What about William and Becca, you were their father and you betrayed them. You failed to protect your beautiful, helpless children."

All at once, deathly imposters of his once wholesome offspring appeared before him. They taunted him to do the unthinkable.

"Avenge us, father."

"Yes... yes..." Regrettably the eccentric scholar had passed over into the realms of complete insanity, and started his quest for vengeance on an already troubled Dawson. He grabbed his fellow traveller and began to strangle him to within an inch of his life.

The ever brave and trusted Sid was sadly unable to help his fallen comrades as he, too, was caught in the evil clutches of The Watchers' terrifying hold. Not with ghosts from his past but with insulting slurs coming from all around him.

"Who's the fairy?" whispered a voice.

"Fairy?" said another.

"Yes, the poor sod over there."

"Fairy? ...Fairy! ...Fairy? ...Fairy! ...Fairy? ...Fairy!" the whispering choir hummed.

Sid gave off an unearthly scream, turning red with sheer anger, and proceeded to attack everything around him, including his faithful companions. All seemed lost.

The shadow of The Watchers started to grow stronger. Their psychological hold ran deeper than before. Darkness engulfed the area where our fallen heroes would face their unspeakable end. That is, until something of a mechanical miracle stumbled out of nowhere.

"Boss!" cried Boris.

"I told you he was here, Boris," said Towser.

"That you did, Towser," said Boris.

The identical robots thus started to shake their creator out of his vile trance. Sullivan was groggy but just about able to become reacquainted with his surroundings.

"Who, who, what, what?" he groaned.

"It's us, boss," said Boris.

"Boris? Towser? How did you both survive?"

"Guess it helped to be fireproof, boss," replied Towser.

"Remarkable," he said, with relief in his voice. "Now help Mr Dawson and Mr Sid immediately!"

The robots followed orders and, after a shake and a shining white light from Boris's eyes, the great butler was finally snatched out of his harrowing prison.

The robots, however, used a slightly more direct approach to break The Watchers' hold over Sid, as Towser proceeded to slap the pixie with both hands.

"Eugh, what's going on?" asked Sid, wearily. "I wasn't out on the dust again, was I?" Suddenly, he looked up to see Towser staring curiously back at him and properly came to.

"Did you have to hit me so hard, you demented rust bucket? I did have everything under control... I think."

"Boris! Towser! Quick, shine the light directly at the silhouettes," shouted Sullivan. The Watchers dispersed instantly, back to their darkly slumber, with nothing more than a silent scowl. In a matter of seconds the nightmare was over.

Dawson wiped the sweat from his forehead while Sid thought it was best to draw on his pipe. "Sully, my friend, next time let's not leave the emotionless robots at home," he said.

This made both Dawson and Sullivan laugh for the first time since crashing into the Forgotten Forest.

"Amen to that," said Sullivan.

"What about Amelia?" asked Dawson. "Is there any sign of her?"

Sullivan and Sid's mood changed drastically, fearing for the life for their young friend.

"Amelia?" asked Boris, looking slightly bewildered, as only a robot can.

"Oh was that the wee 'un we passed only an hour ago, Boris?" asked Towser, innocently.

"You what?!" screamed Dawson, having a sudden urge to thrash the pair of them into scrap metal.

"It's ok, Mr Butlerman," said Towser. "We know where she's going. Follow us, she can't be far."

"You two had better be right. The fate of the entire Unseen Universe depends on it," said Sullivan, in a reflective manner.

XVI

IT was not long before Amelia settled herself enough after that indescribable ordeal to conjure up a small bronze lantern to help her navigate through the starless cavern of forestry.

The girl probably would have preferred a flashlight like the one she often used back home but it mattered little, so long as she could see more than two feet in front of her. However, more to the point, the lantern was far prettier.

She very carefully crept through a dirt track, paranoid Ulana would snatch her away at any minute, or worse, that that horrid voice would return to haunt her again. There was an unsettling silence throughout the forest.

"GAAAARRGHHHH!"

What was that, she thought? Ulana? The Watchers? Surely it could not be The Mute Sullivan warned her about. Amelia found the nearest bush, or the remnants of a bush, and hid. She started to frantically panic and fluster.

"GAAAAAARRRGHHHH!"

There it was again! The sound was not moving? Amelia was tired of running, and even more tired of being scared. She took a deep breath and cleared her head of all the fear weighing her down. The girl held her lantern up high and went to investigate.

Suffice it to say, the cries of "GAAAAAAAARRRRRGGGHHHH" got louder and louder as Amelia rummaged through the bristles of the crumbling Forgotten Forest. She peeked around from behind a decrepit bush. Much to her astonishment she found not a Watcher, nor Ulana, nor The Mute at all.

"GAAAARRRRRGGGGGHHHHH!"

How strange, Amelia thought. Before her eyes was a beast very similar to a Wolpertinger, the grisly looking yet extremely peaceful and civilised species that lived in the Light of the Unseen World. The brown- and yellow-furred brute was caught in a horribly uncomfortable cage.

Unlike your typical Wolpertinger, this beast had not a monocle, chronicle, waistcoat, umbrella, nor indeed a cane. It did, however, have the customary gruesome, razor sharp teeth and stood approximately ten feet tall. Amelia felt there was good reason it might be locked in that cage. She thought it best to walk away.

"GAAAAAAAAAARRRRRRGGGGHHHHH!"

The girl turned towards the beast once again and held her lantern up to its face. The poor thing was weeping in despair. Not just a curious and wonderful soul, Amelia Black was a kind soul too and felt it was her duty to do the right thing.

"Em, hello there," she said, approaching the cage cautiously. "I don't want to hurt you, I just want to help you from this cage."

From her lantern a spritely little ember leaped to the ground, hopping uncontrollably everywhere, setting small bushes and dead grass alight.

"Now stop that!" said Amelia to the spritely, sentient, little ember. "Please could you melt the lock on that cage? I'm in a bit of a hurry."

The little ember leaped up to the lock and turned a deep, vibrant blue. Within seconds the lock had melted away and the beast broke through the bars, releasing a deafening roar similar to this:

"Rooooooooaaaaaaaaaaaaaaarrrrrrrrrr!"

Then there was an awkward silence, as Amelia stared rather blankly at the beast. "Do you have a name at all?" she asked.

The beast was slightly confused. "Gargh?" it replied.

"Well, nice to meet you... Gargh. My name's Amelia Black."

"Gargh," he nodded.

"Do you know the way to the Malus Mountains? I'm afraid I'm slightly lost."

Gargh thought for a minute. Thought *really* hard. He looked befuddled.

"It's a big scary mountain, at least that's what I'm told. A big, horrid, unpleasant, monster called Ulana lives there," explained Amelia.

Gargh thought some more. This time, he thought even harder than the last. Then all of a sudden, yes that's right, everything magically clicked into place. The beast gave an outlandishly upbeat smile.

"Gargh!" nodded Gargh, while jumping up and down elatedly. Amelia was relieved. Some luck at last, she thought.

The girl held out her hand in friendship and walked with the beast into the depths of the unknown once more.

"You weren't going to eat me, were you?" asked Amelia.

Gargh felt a tad embarrassed and shook his head slowly, hoping the girl would forgive him for putting her in such a state.

"Nargh," said Gargh, softly.

And so, Amelia and her new, rather uncouth friend, Gargh, continued on their way towards the Malus Mountains. Unfortunately the dear heroine still had a long way to go before she was even out of the treacherous clutches of The Forgotten Forest.

XVII

WHILE our heroes bravely navigated the foreboding Forgotten Forest, evil loomed elsewhere. At the centre of an endlessly decrepit labyrinth, in the heart of the perilous Malus Mountains, lay Ulana's fortress.

The scarred and loathsome creature had returned to its slumber after its last encounter with Amelia Black.

The hideous stench of death and despair clouded the chamber of the beast. Hideous whispers and wicked laughter slowly began to echo around the hollow hall. A voice, returned to haunt its heartless minion.

"I LOST HER, MY QUEEN," said Ulana. The beast proceeded to swathe its wounds.

"You fail me yet again," said The Voice.

"SHE GROWS STRONGER," snarled Ulana.

"All you had to do was bring her to this fortress. Was that so hard, you insufferable cretin?"

Ulana could say nothing.

"No matter, everything is set in motion. I visited the girl myself, brought her to her knees. Soon she will come to us, and will do anything I say."

"KILL HER NOW."

"Kill her now?" A multitude of voices, all shapes and sizes, taunted the monster like it was a sideshow freak or a dunce schoolboy. "Ulana, my precious, understand this. You are a blunt, powerful instrument to be delivered with direction and force. In this capacity you have few equals." The beast felt the Voice's presence mature, almost as if she was standing over its shoulder. "But your short-sightedness fails you. Now, do you remember what happened last time, my sweet?" she said.

Ulana's silence was almost as deafening as the lingering cackles conjured by the unseen witch. It stood firm and clutched into the lifeless cold floor beneath its rusted claws. It began to breathe heavily; an unsettling growl.

"Ulana, you know I only do this because I love you," she said. "I would ask you to look me in the eyes when you sulk, but I guess even that would be slightly senseless."

The claws of Ulana started to quiver, the quiver quickly turned into a shudder, then the shudder finally turned into a sharp uncontrollable tremble. Seconds later, the unsettlingly sharp feeling moved through its entire body and brought the monster to within an inch of its life. Emerald tainted blood started to drip on to the chamber floor from its terrifyingly lifeless eyes.

The Voice merely mused while the gigantic monster lay in torment on the ground of its chamber.

"True, I never expected Loren to have the nerve to bring her here, let alone grant her travel into the Dark, but I suppose I did force his hand somewhat."

Ulana continued to scamper frantically, screeching in pain. "GIVE ME ONE MORE CHANCE," it screamed.

"In time," she said. "The girl will make her way through the labyrinth. Only after experiencing the horrors between us will her spirit crumble into dust."

"WHAT ABOUT THE COMPANIONS? I'LL RIP THEM APART ONE BY ONE."

"No. Wait for the girl's arrival, and watch over our other guests. Let Zarin attend to her companions," said The Voice.

XVIII

BACK in the depths of the Forgotten Forest, the intrepid crew of the once great *Blanchard,* consisting of Boris, Towser, Sid, Sullivan and Dawson, set up camp to sort through the salvaged remains of their ship. Sullivan was relieved to find a few flares which would scare off any more of those horrid and foul creatures, The Watchers.

"Do we have any weapons?" asked Dawson.

"I've got a spear," said Sid.

The butler's eyes rolled with frustration. "What I mean to say is, do we have any weapons that are larger than my index finger?"

Sullivan reached into his leather satchel – which was beautifully decorated with mystifying symbols – and lifted out a variety of items. Dawson was sure some of the items could not have fit into the bag whilst in the realms of our own world. However, by this stage little surprised him.

"Ah, here we are, Dawson, this looks like it could be more to your liking," said the scholar. Sullivan presented Dawson with a rifle. How boring, you might say, but this was not just any rifle, this was a quadruple barrel weapon, coated in an inferno glaze (for protection, of course), firing not mere bullets but the one thing those disgusting and malevolent creatures of the Dark hate the most: light.

"It also has a switch at the side which lets you choose the colour of light you wish to fire," explained Sullivan. "Makes no difference in truth, but I've always preferred using orange. I like orange. Now there's a colour. Energy, warmth, calmness," he mused.

An awkward silence fell between Dawson, Sid and the robots, at Sullivan's faintly eccentric reminiscing.

"You're weird sometimes, y'know that, Sully?" said Sid.

"Hm? What?" asked Sullivan.

"I think we'd better just get moving, don't you?" asked Dawson.

As an eerie fog descended throughout the forest, Dawson, though in the company of kind, right-minded gentlemen, was beginning to feel scared. The last encounter with The Watchers was still fresh in his mind. That harrowing illusion of Aoibhinn Black taunting him for losing Amelia troubled him greatly.

"Boris, Towser," said Sullivan, "do you have a fix on the girl's location?" The robots were operating peculiar scanning devices, almost like a pocket watch located inside their forearms but with a compass-like tracking system.

"We think so, boss," said Boris.

"We know so, boss," explained Towser.

"Due north," said Boris.

"I have due south," said Towser.

"No, Towser, you're just reading it upside down, adjust your optics," moaned Boris.

Towser did just that.

"Right you are, Boris," said Towser.

"Hm. Curious," said Sullivan, examining Boris' tracking system.

"What's wrong?" asked Dawson. His mood tightened. "Has something happened to her? Please..."

"Well, it's hard to know, but it seems to indicate she is with someone... or more likely, some*thing*," said Sullivan.

A harsh wind cut through the unforgiving forest.

"Let's go," said Dawson.

"Hang on, who died and made you the King?" said Sid.

"No one, but out there right now is an 11-year-old girl, in a horrifying forest, lost, maybe seriously hurt or just unimaginably frightened to death." Dawson grabbed Sid in his hand. The pixie could see the blazing fire of rage and frustration melting from Dawson's face. "Now, we either go *right now*, or you can stay here and I will go to save the only person in my life currently worth a damn. Then I'm going to those infernal mountains to save the other two people. Understand?"

All were silent. The pixie squeezed himself out of Dawson's hand, blushing slightly. "Well, I guess when you put it like that..." said Sid.

Dawson threw down his jacket, rolled up his shirt sleeves and continued walking, his newly acquired rifle in hand. Sullivan, Sid and the two robots could only admire the butler's courage and slight foolishness and proceeded to follow suit. The wind-chill increased as they walked further away from the wreckage of their ship and deeper into the darkness of the Forgotten Forest.

There was a scuffling sound amongst the trees. Deep bellowing sounds surrounded the crew.

"The Watchers again?" asked Dawson.

"I... don't know," said Sullivan.

Suddenly, Boris was snatched into the shadows, without so much as a whisper.

"Boss..." said Towser.

"Not now. I'm trying to think." said Sullivan.

"But boss..." and then, in a flash, Towser was snatched away too.

The bellowing sound erupted again. Without warning, one of the lifeless trees snatched at Sullivan's legs. Dawson tried to help him, stuck in a hopeless exercise of tug-o-war. The tree's wickedness soon spread, as it attempted to snatch at the butler as well.

"The rifle, Dawson!" screamed Sullivan.

Dawson acted accordingly but before he could fire the first beam the object was knocked out of his hands. He made a dive for his weapon, while the twisting, bone-like branches attempted to snatch at him also.

Sid tried to act fast. Being familiar with treefolk he launched himself at the heart of the tree, flying fast and true, but was unable to breach the seemingly indestructible bark.

Dawson was clinging on to the ground for dear life, trying to crawl through the dirt; the rifle merely inches away. He tugged with a thud, and slammed with a wham, closer and closer. With all his might he jumped for his weapon and showed that wicked tree the light.

What was quite extraordinary, however, was not the tree ceasing all dangerous activity, but that by shooting the beam of light – which Dawson set to *'Rainbow Mode'* – it restored the tree to life, blossoming lush, emerald leaves and emanating a luminous glow.

It was not long before Boris and Towser came bumbling out of the darkness.

"Well, that was unexpected," said Boris.

"Very much so, Boris," said Towser.

Sid and Dawson quickly regrouped. Sullivan, meanwhile, was dazzled by the sight before him.

"Fascinating," thought Sullivan. "It appears that using the light beam has restored the objects to their natural state of being, their 'true colours' if you will." The good scholar had heard rumours, myths, and legends of such events but had never had the chance to see it happen with his own eyes.

Before the rest were able to properly appreciate the beauty in the dark, I fear events simply got worse. There were several scuttles and creeps and crawls. The group froze. From the shadows emerged hundreds of mechanical creatures which looked faintly reminiscent of the large spiders Dawson often found in the depths of the Black's wine cellar.

Dawson fired the rifle once again but it was no use; it seemed to have little effect on non-organic life. He quickly resorted to kicking them away, but that did not work either; the spiders grew in numbers and swarmed over the butler. Sid tried his best to combat them with his lance but he too could only handle so much at a time. Sullivan looked as though he was beyond saving. Already the spiders had cocooned him within their web.

The butler tried to resist but he and the robots fell to a similar fate. Sid could do nothing but retreat, for he knew if there was a way to save his friends he must first find Amelia.

XIX

COMPARED to recent events, Amelia and her new, beastly-looking friend Gargh had been wandering through The Forgotten Forest with minimal fuss. Though rough around the edges, Gargh was smart enough to know where to wander within the forest, and where to avoid.

Crossing over the rickety Bridge of Torment, located above the eerie Lagoon of Disenchantment, they even sneakily avoided the house of the creature whose name no one should speak – mainly because no one has ever survived to actually find out its name.

"So, Gargh, tell me about yourself," said Amelia.

"Gargh," replied Gargh. The friendly beast was not really sure what to say or do. No one had ever cared enough – or indeed been brave enough – to ask dear Gargh to talk about himself before.

"Well, do you have a mother or a father?" she continued. "Oh, what about your friends? I'm sure someone like you has all kinds of different friends here."

Amelia's wide-eyed and curious enthusiasm rarely ceased to amaze, even in the most dangerous of locations. A look of awkwardness fell upon Gargh's furry face, as he shook his head once more.

"Nobody at all?" she asked. "Everyone has at least one friend. Guess I'm really lucky to have Dawson and Sid and Mr Sullivan and I suppose Boris and Towser, too."

There was a prolonged yet serene silence. The beast did not need to think hard, or even at all this time, all he did was simply point to Amelia.

"Me?" she asked.

"Gargh!" the beast nodded enthusiastically.

Amelia felt humbled by Gargh's declaration and gave her furry friend a huge hug.

"So how much further until we are out of this silly forest?" she asked.

Gargh, not one for being the most articulate, weighed up the distance with his hands. "Gargh," he mused.

"So we'll finally be out of here soon?" she asked with a hint of relief and delight.

"Gargh," said Gargh.

"Thank goodness," said Amelia. Already she could see the cluttered distribution of the gloomy and lifeless trees thinning out. One step closer to saving her mother and father, she thought.

The silence of the forest was broken by faint cries.

"Amelia..."

Amelia started to become tense, hiding behind Gargh's furry and ferocious figure. The cries got louder.

"Ameliaaa..."

It was getting closer!

"Ameliaaaaaa!"

And in the blink of an eye Sid crashed through the nearby trees, panting in exhaustion, flustered from the search for his lost friend.

"Sid!" screamed Amelia in delight. "How did you find me? Are you alright?" She picked her friend up carefully within the palm of her grubby hands.

"Ah... thank the Light... just, just give me a moment." The pixie tried to straighten himself out, adjusting his shabby waistcoat accordingly. "Some pixie dust would go down well right about now."

Amelia being the kind-hearted soul we have come to know, dutifully obliged her companion with her best conjure of Pixie Dust for his elaborately designed pipe. He buried the dust into the pipe, lit it up, and the strange purple glow was emitted once more.

"It's not quite Fáfnir quality, but it's not half bad," he concluded.

"Sid! Oh, I'm so relieved to see you," said Amelia. She looked around, slightly confused not to see the rest of her friends. "But where are Dawson and the others?"

The Pixie's faced was stricken with fear and guilt.

"I should have done more," he said. "I should have stayed and tried to save them."

Amelia assumed the worst, but remained as calm as possible. "Are they... lost?" she asked.

Sid brooded in silence for a minute. "No," he said firmly. "But we can't waste any time, the spiders have taken them to The Mother."

Gargh, who had been quiet up until now, started to panic uncontrollably.

"Gargh, settle down!" said Amelia.

"Hey!" said Sid. "Who's the Wolpertinger?" The pixie was quite fascinated by the beast.

"Oh yes, of course. Sid, this is Gargh, he's been helping me navigate through the forest. I saved him from a trap!" she declared proudly.

"Good to have you along for the ride, Gargh," said Sid.

"Gargh!" roared Gargh.

"Now, now, no need to be like that. Anyone who is a friend of Amelia's is a friend of mine. Except maybe Boris and Towser."

"That's not very nice, Sid," said Amelia.

"Just saying. Right, Gargh, fancy directing us to The Mother's lair?"

Gargh appeared reluctant at first, but nodded in agreement, "gargh." And so the trio headed east through the bleak outskirts of The Forgotten Forest.

"I like your style," said Sid.

"Gargh."

"Ah, don't be too hard on the lass, she's new to these parts," said Sid.

"Excuse me?" said Amelia.

"Oh, um, never mind, pixie/wolpertinger stuff..." explained Sid.

Gargh and Sid went ahead as Amelia fell slightly behind. Darkness started to surround the girl. She had felt this cold breathing feeling lurking in the shadows before. Familiar whispers clouded her mind once again.

"So, to The Mother's lair you go, my dear?" said The Voice. "Now that's bold. Why would you even bother? Your friends are useless and could almost certainly be dead already. Especially that butler, what a weak soul he is."

"Shut up!" screamed Amelia. "Go away! I hate you!" The tears streamed down her face. Despite her unquestionable courage since their first encounter, The Voice still had a chilling hold over her. Then the darkness dispersed and she was back with Sid and Gargh again.

"Alright, I apologise, we didn't mean to exclude you from our enchanted citizen babble..." said Sid. "Though 'hate' is a little harsh..."

"I'm sorry, I'm not sure what's come over me..." said Amelia.

"Well, come on, Gargh says the lair is barely half a day's walk from here. We should save Dawson, Sully and the dumbots by supper, all being well," said Sid.

"Gargh," said Gargh.

"Look, I just said that, please do keep up," said Sid to his furry friend.

Under the bone white moon they travelled through the night... or day... no one is ever quite sure in these troubled lands.

One last time The Voice returned to taunt Amelia with another, more chilling, threat. It whispered softly, "I'll be seeing you soon, my pet, very *very* soon."

Amelia tried to ignore it, but The Voice kept on whispering to the girl. "Oh, and if you utter a single word about me to any of your friends, I'll turn all of them into dust, in the blink of an eye."

All Amelia could do was keep quiet; too much was at stake.

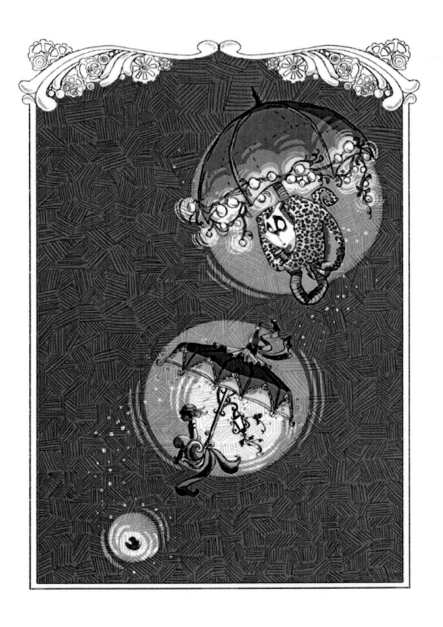

XX

THE hours passed exceedingly slowly as Amelia and Sid, led by their latest companion, emerged from the nerve-jangling and claustrophobic surroundings of The Forgotten Forest. Those haunting final words that the cruel and merciless voice uttered to the girl were still nesting in her thoughts.

They passed beyond the forest's clutches. Below them was a seemingly bottomless canyon separating them from the inner regions of the Dark. Across the chasm, in the distance under the pale moonlight, they could see the unusual Malus Mountains.

"That is where I must go," thought Amelia. But she had a responsibility to her friends, especially Dawson. Though her father cared for her very much, even she knew Dawson was the person who truly raised her, taught her right from wrong, and would risk his own life for her's without even a second thought.

"Gargh,"

"Down there?" asked Sid, pointing to the canyon. The beast nodded.

"But how will we get down there?" asked Amelia. The girl peeked over the edge, all she could see was a dark, chilling mist. In the distance there were faint screams; perhaps they were already too late, she thought. She even kept expecting that detestable voice to appear again to haunt her. But it didn't.

"Well, I can fly. You and Gargh will have to use your imagination," said Sid.

Amelia thought for a minute and then closed her eyes. Within seconds she had conjured her most ideal gliding device.

"An umbrella, Amelia?" said Sid, slightly disappointed. "Couldn't think a little bigger? What about poor Gargh here. His weight..."

"GARGH!"

"No need to get so touchy, Gargh, you're just significantly bigger than both of us. Look, from my perspective even Amelia is a giant. Or a giant girl's little doll, at least."

Sid had upset Gargh enormously, and the beast began to sulk on the dirty ground. The pixie was not aware how sensitive the beast was about his weight.

"Oh no, I'm so sorry, Gargh," said Amelia. The girl gave her hairy companion another hug, like she would her favourite teddy bear on her bed. "Okay, I think I can fix this." She remembered what Loren said to her in the Chamber of Thoughts, about making her objects more than what they seemed. So she held the umbrella up high and made the item expand and strengthen. Just to give it her own touch, she added vibrant, sparklingly fairy lights set against its pure black design.

"Hmm, not bad, but the visuals are a bit uncalled for," said Sid.

"Well, I think they're pretty," said Amelia, cheerfully.

"Gargh," nodded Gargh.

"See?" said Amelia. "Even Gargh likes them."

"Alright, fine, let's just hurry. One, two, three... vamoose!" The pixie glided himself down the sinister dark space, careful not to make any sort of sound.

Amelia tidied her hair into a small pony tail, using a simple purple ribbon. The girl had strict lessons drilled into her at a very young age, oddly by Dawson moreso than her mother, to always look clean and tidy regardless of the occasion or how mundane the location may seem. However, she did not think Dawson ever meant for life or death situations in horrifying spiders' nests.

"You ready, Gargh?" asked Amelia.

The big friendly beast looked at his gliding device carefully, not entirely sure how it worked.

"It's fine, you just push that button above the handle, like this." And so to demonstrate, the girl launched her umbrella and Gargh, always a fast learner, quickly followed his friend's lead. "Now, are you ready?"

"Gargh," nodded Gargh.

"Gargh, I'm scared," said Amelia.

There was a measured silence. Amelia took a deep breath. She closed her eyes. Then she leaped into the vast darkness below.

Now, it goes without saying that the dangers that awaited Amelia and her friends were fairly horrific. However, for those brief moments, while falling into this unforgiving canyon, Amelia felt lighter than air and more free than all the creatures in the Seen and Unseen realms.

Gargh, however, was clinging on to his umbrella for dear life, closing his eyes hard and refusing to look down.

As Amelia dropped deeper and deeper into the abyss, the mist was unbearable. She could barely see her hands mere inches in front of her face. There were sounds of creepy crawlies up and down the chamber, echoing all around her.

After they eventually breached the layer of mist, a soft glow filled the chamber. Amelia noticed grotesque red ooze with a horrible odour dripping from holes on either side of her. Rapidly the canyon began to shrink. The walls werengetting narrower and narrower, until poor Gargh was having trouble fitting comfortably down the shaft.

"Don't be frightened, Gargh, we're surely bound to hit the ground soon," said Amelia. She started to wonder about Sid, and yelled out his name.

"Help me!" cried Sid, frantically.

"Sid, where are you?" yelled Amelia.

"Um, ever heard the one about the spider that caught the fly? I don't mean to alarm anyone right now, but I'm the bloody fly!" said Sid, calm and collected as always.

Amelia floated further down to find the pixie trapped on a nearby ledge in a spider's web, as one of the mechanical creatures that had abducted their friends earlier slowly stalked him, ready to strike its rusty, jagged pincers into his miniscule body.

"Do something!" cried the pixie.

Amelia quickly conjured the only object she could think of on the spot, a glass jar.

"A jar?!" said Sid, inches from death. "Great, fine, good, slam it, smash it, just kill it!"

The girl panicked as she trapped the mechanical creature in the jar, and threw the jar into the red ooze seeping from the walls of the vent.

"Thank the Light," said Sid.

The girl pulled her tiny friend from the gooey remains of the web.

Sid was repulsed by the state his clothes had been left in. "This will take weeks to get out," he moaned.

Amelia, however, was happy to placate Sid with a new pair of crimson coloured trousers, white shirt and black waistcoat. "Are you ok, Sid?" she asked.

"Yeah, I'll be alright," he said. "I've been through worse anyway. Remind me to tell you the tale of the time I battered the ugly trolls of Carpenter's Swamp. Oh, they'll be talking about that one for centuries to come." He managed to pull his spear out of the sticky remains of the web. "Come on, judging from the ooze on the walls and the horrible stench of..." he put his nose in the air and nearly turned green with disgust, "...death, I'd say we're near the bottom."

So our fearless rescuers travelled the remaining depths of the cavern, and landed in absolute darkness. The stench was becoming unbearable. Amelia conjured three gas masks to help them from throwing up at the wretched smell.

"I can't see in this thing," said Sid, "it's too dark." He decided to rest on Gargh's shoulder for this portion of the journey, feeling slightly weak and woozy from his encounter with the horrid spider.

Suddenly there was an uncomfortable clicking sound, breaking through the silence. The frantic pattering sound of insect legs started to surround them.

"One second, I'll just give us some light..."

"No, Amelia, don't!" cried Sid.

It was already too late. Amelia filled the battered shaft with a warm light, only to find hundreds of the spiders staring at them menacingly.

"Run, Gargh!" shouted Sid. Despite his hefty exterior, Gargh picked up the girl in his left arm and burst down the shaft at lightning speed. Giving a battle cry, the beast fended off countless mechanical monstrosities that got in his way.

"I'm not sure how much longer the big guy can take this, Amelia," said Sid in a panicked tone.

"I've got an idea," said Amelia brightly. "Stop here, Gargh."

The beast did as it was told, though Sid was screaming profanities at his young leader's unorthodox decision. Gargh let Amelia go and she stood ahead of her friends. The spiders were fast approaching them, readying themselves to dig their rusty claws into their flesh.

"I hope this works," thought Amelia.

Within moments a rupturing sound filled the creaky insides of the tunnel. For a brief moment everything stopped. A blazing inferno of sun-fire eradicated all the spiders in its path. Amelia stood strong and waved her hands, making the blaze surround Sid, Gargh and herself. All that remained were the lifeless, charred remains of the vicious insects. Amelia passed out, drained and hurting from using her powers to such great effect.

Gargh picked her up once more and followed Sid down the darkened shaft. Sid looked concerned but relieved to survive yet another death-defying encounter.

"The girl did good," he whispered.

"Gargh," nodded Gargh in agreement.

"Hopefully that's the majority of the minions destroyed," said Sid. "Though The Mother is going to be very angry."

Creeping carefully through the shadows, Sid, Gargh, and a drained Amelia Black continued down the mines, edging closer to The Mother's lair.

XXI

AFTER a drawn-out period of navigating carefully through the narrow shaft, Sid, Gargh, and an unconscious Amelia Black – resting on the beast's shoulder – came to a puzzling crossroads.

Before them were five entrances. Giant archways, unsurprisingly surrounded by haggard cobwebs and copious amounts of that ghastly red ooze they passed through earlier.

"Which way though?" thought Sid. "Got anything, Gargh?" he asked out loud.

"Gargh," said Gargh.

"Hmm, I was thinking through the middle also," said Sid.

"Gargh..."

"I was, too!" said Sid. "Look, forget whose idea it was. Can we just continue on?"

And so, by way of no apparent logic, they walked through the central entrance and everything seemed normal.

"I... guess... this is the right way?" said Sid.

A deathly chill passed through the cavern. Sid flew just ahead of Gargh, his light guiding the way.

"See? What did I tell you? Nothing to worry about," said Sid.

As they approached the end of the tunnel, the pixie noticed a strange red glow. They found themselves standing once again in front of five entrances nearly identical to the previous ones.

"Coincidence?" mused Sid out loud.

"Gargh." The beast did not sound impressed.

Moments later Amelia woke up, still feeling groggy from the earlier events. She rubbed her eyes, just like she would if waking up from the gentle comfort of her warm bed. "What's going on?" she asked.

"Well, we're not quite sure, but we think we might be lost," explained Sid. "But as I said, we're not quite sure."

Amelia looked closely at the entry ways, staring into the blackness.

"What if we just go through the middle?" asked Amelia.

"We tried that while you were asleep. We walked down a long dark corridor and suddenly ended up back in front of the exact same caves."

Amelia fell on her behind, conjuring a little wooden seat to catch her fall. Her power was growing, and she did not even realise it.

"Gargh,"

"Eh?" said Sid. "That couldn't have been important to our current situation."

"What did Gargh say?" asked Amelia, standing up from her seat looking ever so curious.

"Well, when we emerged from the cave the first time there was some strange red light shining all around us, but frankly I don't think that matters much."

Gargh, like many of our heroes before him, was starting to get deeply frustrated by the pixie's ignorance.

"GARGH!!" screamed the beast. Some of Gargh's growly phlegm covered Sid. For once he was at a loss for words.

Amelia walked past each entrance one more time.

"Well, in my world, there are these cryptic tunnels in huge pyramids," said Amelia. "My parents used to tell me how they would spend hours at a time trying to figure out the right way to where the hidden treasure was buried. Maybe the red light means we're going the wrong way?"

Sid was frantically cleaning Gargh's gunk off his clothes, trying his best not to vomit from the smell, and looked up to find Amelia and Gargh staring awkwardly at him.

"Well, perhaps," said Sid. The pixie flew around as fast as pixie-ly possible to dry himself off, and then continued, "but we don't have the time! Dawson and Sullivan's lives could depend on it!"

"*And* Boris and Towser!" cried Amelia.

"Yeah, them too," sighed Sid.

"Gargh?" asked Gargh.

"Don't worry, you won't like them. Ignorant mechanical folk."

The beast looked slightly perplexed, and grunted appropriately.

"Sid!" moaned Amelia. "Stop that right now, this is serious."

"But I was being serious," said Sid. "Anyway, back to the point for a minute. Unless we get these mystifying caves right the first time, it could take us hours to try each one."

Amelia mused for a minute and then magically presented four mini star lanterns, similar to the objects she saw in The Amalricus Room back at Loren's castle. "Okay, now I just need to change three of their colours."

And so the remaining bright white stars became yellow, blue and purple. Sid closely examined the objects, particularly curious to see what Amelia would do next.

"Now we take these star lanterns and throw them down each entry and whichever one doesn't return back to us surely must be the right way," explained Amelia.

Sid was suitably impressed by his companion's playful inventiveness.

Gargh, however, was simply over-excited and proceeded to give Amelia a hug. This made Amelia smile. "I hope this works," she said. "One, two, three, go!"

Off like a flash, the star lanterns zoomed down each entry way. The white down the far left, the blue beside it, they skipped the middle and proceed to throw the sun-like yellow down the inside right and, last but not least, the purple lantern went shooting down the far right. And then, they waited.

The pixie lit up his pipe, when suddenly Gargh roared with delight as the blue, yellow and white lights came zooming towards them.

"So the purple light is where we're going, brilliant!" said Sid. "But, uh, which entrance did we throw the purple one down?"

"Gargh."

"Are you sure? You were the one who made us go down the middle originally!"

The beast remained silent as tension between the pair grew.

"It doesn't matter whose idea it was," said Amelia. "It's the one at the end." The girl stormed off down the entrance on the far right. Gargh and Sid dutifully followed.

As they reached the middle of the cave, bizarre things started to happen. All the walls within the cave began to morph into black and white chequered squares, similar to the type found on a chessboard.

"Maybe it's redecorating?" said Sid.

They crept with caution and came forward to find themselves upside-down, walking through an immense and complex stairwell.

"Now this is just getting silly..." the pixie said.

Amelia looked up – or down, even – and saw a light at the very top.

"That's where we've got to go," she said.

"Something tells me your star-lanterns aren't going to get us out of this one," said Sid.

"Gargh," added Gargh.

"It'll take forever to navigate through those stairs without Mr Sullivan helping us," said Amelia. "We're just going to have to rocket ourselves up, up and away."

"How original," said Sid, in a dry tone.

"Be quiet, Sid," said Amelia forcefully.

Sid was surprised by his friend's reaction, thinking it was perhaps time to scale back the wit for more relaxed occasions. "I'm sorry, that was rude of me. Please continue." His willingness to admit he was in the wrong comforted the girl.

"Okay, Gargh, since you're the strongest you're going to be our pilot for my latest invention!" The beast was curious. Within seconds Amelia conjured a steam propelled pack with a rotor sticking out two meters from the top base.

"Gargh," said Gargh in awe.

"The stairwell is too narrow for any huge machine, like The Blanchard, but a personal flying machine is bound to work," said Amelia.

Gargh strapped himself in. Amelia even gave the furry beast her own goggles which fitted rather tightly around his larger head. That did not seem to trouble Gargh though.

"Ready?" asked Amelia.

"Gargh!" The friendly monster held onto Amelia firmly, as they raise themselves off the ground and towards the top of the long and intricate duct.

"We're nearly there!" shouted Amelia. And then...

SPLAT!

The three were trapped in a large oozing spider's web. Amelia was trying her hardest to imagine something, anything that might force them out of this trap. A knife, perhaps even a spike? All seemed useless. Then a dark, distorted figure stood over the pit, where the spider's web lay.

"Well, well, well," a weak, disturbing, male voice said. "It seems the spider has caught a couple of large flies. And a little fairy."

"Pixie," said Sid, trying his best to free himself from this web of horror.

"Whatever. She said you would come, Ms Black," said the dark figure. "I have to admit, I didn't think you would get through my twisted little maze, but she always had faith.

"Who?" said Amelia. "The Mother?"

"The Mother? Don't be preposterous! I *am* The Mother." The figure crept into the light to reveal a frail-looking man in a white doctor's uniform, with long, black hair and flamboyant make-up. He crept forward a little more to reveal the rest of his wretched, disgusting body to be the hind parts of a giant spider. Amelia went pale, wanting to vomit at the sight of him.

The grotesque creature smiled at the child's reaction, spitting a sort of venom in her and her companions' eyes, knocking them out cold. "Now, where were we?" the monster whispered

to itself.

XXII

AMELIA eventually came out of the comatose state to find herself trapped in another web, on her own, in an intensely warm yet dim-lit room. The room itself looked like a cluttered, confused workshop, similar to the specialised variety steam engineers would use to assemble all kinds of weird and wonderful devices back in her realm. The girl could faintly see the grotesque figure of The Mother in the dim light – working away with all six of his arms fixing his mechanical monstrosities.

"I never used to be like this, you know," said the creature. "The Mother isn't even my name. It's more a title I acquired over the years for constructing my beautiful creations. My beautiful creations that that soulless cretin, Loren, rejected." He picked up a hammer by its scraped and battered bronze handle, with his middle right hand, and slammed this peculiar blue device into the base of his latest mechanical spider. "Perfect," he continued. "Oh, yes, my name: Zarin Glass. It's been a lifetime since anyone has referred to me by that name."

Amelia was feeling weak, coughing intensely, unable to concentrate on conjuring anything which could help her out of this sticky predicament.

"I know what you're trying to do, Ms Black. Trust me when I say you're wasting your time," said the frail, creepy, skin-crawling creature. "I've injected you with mild paralysing venom. It won't kill you but it will affect your train of thought enough to..."

Suddenly The Mother became distracted, shifting its conversation to itself. "What's that?" it said. "Yes, certainly, I wasn't going... but I mean... of course... she'll be ready once I've... no her friends aren't... I see."

Amelia was not sure if The Mother was simply disturbed or perhaps talking to someone more familiar to the girl already.

"'Hat 'as her in't it," mumbled Amelia. "The awful wman who could do ba' tings from far."

Zarin's attention broke. His twisted body crawled rapidly towards Amelia. It looked her straight in the eyes. "You really are a curious soul," said the monster. "Only 'Children of the Dark' can hear *her* voice." The Mother gave an uncomfortable grin. "Tell me, Amelia, how black is your heart?"

Amelia was struggling to form coherent words. "Wo is 'he?" she asked. "Whee r y frinds?"

"Ah ah ah! Only one question at a time."

"Wat?" said the girl.

"Only one question. Didn't that stupid butler of yours teach you any manners?"

The poor girl was becoming inaudible now, falling unconscious once more.

Meanwhile, down in the cold dark depths of the dungeon lay six webbed cocoons of various sizes. Several of Zarin's spiders circled them, silently stalking in case one were to hatch.

The nerve-jangling silence was broke by the smallest of hatchlings, tossing and turning, trying to force its way out. One of the spiders went to red alert, bringing the near frozen shell down. The mechanical creature examined the shell closely, then attempted to dig its rusted, razor-sharp legs into it.

SLASH.

The spider just had a spear launched straight into its power source, extinguishing all signs of life. Within seconds Sid emerged, slightly pale but no less ill-mannered. "I'm really starting to hate spiders," he declared. Within moments the courageous pixie had torn the rest of the wretched machines to pieces, using his speed and absolute rage to fuel him.

He then proceeded to cut his friends down. Gargh's being the biggest pod of the bunch.

"GARGH!" he roared in defiance.

"Too late, I already took care of them," said Sid.

"Gargh," moaned Gargh.

"Quit your sulking and help me release my friends."

And so the Wolpertinger and the pixie cut down the web-encrusted shells with swift force and astonishing precision.

First out of the pod was Dawson, as pale as Sid and twice as disorientated. "What's going on? Where am I?" he asked.

"It's alright, Dawson. Gargh and I are here to save you," said Sid.

"You and who?"

"Gargh," explained Gargh. The beast then politely helped the faithful butler up from the ground and held him carefully to make sure he did not fall back down again.

Next down was Sullivan. Just like the butler, feeling a little bewildered.

"You okay, Sully?" asked Sid.

"Fascinating, truly fascinating. Remind me to document this experience when we're back at the castle. Remarkable..."

"He's fine," said Sid to himself. "Right, quick, let's get out of here and save Amelia!"

"Amelia?" said Dawson. "She's alive? Here? Where?"

"We must hurry, who knows what The Mother will do to her..."

And so Sid galvanised his friends into action. Weaponless though they were, their strength and spirit was never in doubt.

"Wait!" screamed Sullivan.

"What?" asked Sid. "What's wrong?"

"Someone needs to release Boris and Towser!"

Collectively, Dawson and Sid rolled their eyes.

"Do we have to?" moaned the pixie.

Gargh, having never met Boris and Towser, was particularly confused – moreso than usual – regarding the group's current predicament.

"Need I remind you, Mr Sid, of the incident with The Watchers?" said the scholar, trying to clean the encrusted web off his suit.

Sid groaned once again, but knew the scholar had a point and dutifully helped the robots from their encrusted prison.

"Where are we, Towser?" asked Boris.

"Not sure, Boris," said Towser.

"Right, we don't have time for this, let's go. The girl is in real danger!" cried Sid.

However, danger soon crept up on Amelia's friends as countless more spiders burst through the dungeon doors, cornering our heroes into the darkest depths of the room. Sid and Gargh sliced, stabbed and battered them away as the others tried to regain their strength. It was futile as, like their first encounter in The Forgotten Forest, countless drones kept flooding the chamber. It was no use, they thought.

Until something completely extraordinary happened. A troop of brightly lit warriors crashed through the walls and devoured their darkened foes into oblivion.

"Oh no..." said Sid.

"What now?" said Dawson. "More spiders?"

"Worse," said Sid. "Fairies." The pixie attempted to hide himself so he would not be seen by the fairies.

Once the last of the spiders was eliminated, the troop's leader settled down to talk to our near-fallen heroes.

"Alright, ladies, settle down and finish up please, we are in a bit of a rush," said the minuscule female. "Sullivan, sir, are you alright? The King sent us when word got out regarding Zarin."

"We're fine, Maria, thank you for your assistance. I'm not sure I could have handled another session in those diabolical prisons," said Sullivan, still coughing up bits of web. "But how did the King know?"

"Is everyone accounted for?" she asked. "What of the girl?"

"We were just about to go to save her until you lot showed up," said Sid, cutting into the conversation.

"Of course you were, Sidney," said Maria.

"Less of it, Mary," said Sid.

"We can deal with this later. Amelia is up there somewhere," said Dawson.

The intrepid crew of *The Blanchard* – Dawson, Sullivan, Boris, Towser and Sid – managed to retrieve their weapons from a locked chest outside their dungeon cell. So the strange fellowship of bite-sized warriors, two deeply confused robots, the King's personal aide and royal scholar, the Black family's butler and a wolpertinger named Gargh stormed the corridors of the sick and twisted lair into Zarin's main chamber.

The mob burst into the hall to find it ransacked and deserted.

"We're too late," said Dawson.

"Not too late," said a warped voice from the darkness. "Just in time." Zarin emerged from the shadows, mutated into a complete insect form, tossing, turning and smashing everything in his path.

The legion of fairies tried to distract it while Sid went in for the killer blow. Sullivan and the robots could do little but take cover and watch on. Dawson shot a beam of light at Zarin, which threw the monster off as it crashed into the fire slowly burning at the back of the chamber.

The blaze erupted into the room as the monster made a slash for Dawson. The butler ran frantically under the spider's body and picked up a razor sharp leg found on the remains of one of his mechanical subjects. He then stabbed the leg straight into the heart of the grotesque creature and watched as it morphed back into the frail man once more.

Dawson stood over Zarin, "where is Amelia?"

Zarin coughed up some blood and laughed in his face.

"She has her now, and there's nothing you can do to stop her," said Zarin.

"Who has her? Ulana? Speak, damn you," said Dawson.

Zarin laughed uncomfortably once more. "You really have no idea you pathetic, powerless human. All this has been foreseen, the girl is the final piece of the puzzle. Finally the Dark will consume the Unseen Universe once more. Even if you and your friends manage to get out of here alive, there's no way you'll make it to the castle in the mountains in time." Zarin laughed for the last time, a laugh which turned into a cough, a cough which... stopped. So, with a whimper rather than a bang, Zarin Glass, known infamously as 'The Mother,' to all who feared him, took his last breath in the Unseen Universe.

"He was unfortunately right," said Sullivan. "I'm not sure what type of magic Zarin used to whisk Amelia off to the Malus Mountains, but we're still days away, at least."

"Not so, old friend," said Gargh.

The whole room spun round in shock and amazement at the beast's new-found ability to speak.

"Um, what did you just say, Gargh?" asked Sid.

"Forgive me. Excuse the charade for just one moment."
Gargh started to morph into a man. Not just any man, none
other than the King of the Unseen Light himself, Loren.

"Your majesty! How can this be?" asked Sullivan.

"The King is... Gargh? Gargh is... the King? I feel so
used," mumbled Sid.

"Once I got word that *The Blanchard* had crashed on
the border, I decided to take matters into my own hands and
seek out the girl," said Loren. "Obviously had I entered in my
own form I would've attracted needless attention, but a stray
wolpertinger tends to go unnoticed."

"Inspired, sire," said Sullivan.

"Quite," said Dawson. "However, Amelia is now in
grave danger and we have no way of getting to the
mountains."

"Not so," said Loren. The King conjured a darkened
door with cryptic symbols decorating it, quite effortlessly,
similar to the type found in his own castle. "I can't navigate

you straight to the fortress as my powers cannot go there, however, I can guide you to the door of the labyrinth."

The troop of fairies stayed behind to guide the King safely back to the Light. Loren replenished the crew's supplies as they silently entered the door, wary of the dangers that lurked beyond. Braver men would have faltered at the thought, but these men, machines and pixie alike knew there lay a little girl who needed them, as much as they needed her.

XXIII

THE doziness finally passed and Amelia woke up to find herself staring at a bitter and callous grey-stone wall inside the labyrinth of the Malus Mountains. How did she get here? Where were her friends? Were they even alive? What of the sadistic Zarin Glass? Perhaps the darkly presence in the form of that horrid voice brought her here, but she refused to wait around to find out.

She walked around aimlessly finding no hint of logic to the layout of the maze. There seemed to be little indication of any life within the maze, just like the rest of the Dark. The sky was a chilling dark blue, with a solitary ray of moonlight shining upon her.

Amelia conjured herself a compass but it seemed to have little effect as the bronze object continuously span round and round, never looking likely to actually stop. Particularly curious, however, was that any time our dear heroine tried to jump or use anything to propel herself into the air to see where exactly Ulana's castle was located, the walls kept rising higher and higher. It was no use, she thought.

"Having fun yet, my dear?" asked The Voice.

"Go away," said Amelia.

"Well, if you're going to be like that." And strangely The Voice ceased.

She walked cautiously down one of the many passageways littered with gargoyle statues, each as gruesome as the next. She thought she was going mad for a moment, until she heard a few of them speak amongst themselves.

"Who's that?" said one gargoyle, looking like a cross between a devil and a griffin.

"Is she local?" asked another.

"Well she's hardly bloody local now, is she? How many well-dressed little human girls do you see wandering this forsaken hole on a regular basis?" the first one retorted. "I mean, look at her, she's not even made of stone."

"Maybe she's one of those modern models from the most southern reaches of the labyrinth."

"Maybe you're just an idiot."

Amelia overheard the gargoyles' peculiar argument and thought it might be wise to ask if they were aware of the right direction to Ulana's castle.

"I say, you there, little girl!"

Amelia turned and faced the stone statue, not quite sure how to respond. "Um, excuse me, sir?" said the girl.

"Yes, you, what brings you to our humble and crumbled surroundings?"

"So sorry to trouble you, but you wouldn't happen to know how to get to the castle at the centre of this maze at all?"

"Wow, she speaks! And rather well," said the first gargoyle. "How quaint."

"Can she sing?" the other asked.

"Can you si... wait now, what kind of stone-headed question is that?"

"I heard they all tend to break into song occasionally."

"I'm sorry, I am in a bit of a hurry," said Amelia, timidly.

"Of course, forgive my associate; his mind seems to have eroded over the past few millennia. If memory serves me right you keep going down this passage, take the second left then the third right, and enter through the middle archway – you can't miss it, it's a little ostentatious – and the castle should be straight ahead," said the first one.

"Thank you, for being ever so kind, sir," said Amelia. "I'm off to save my mother and father," she concluded. And so she left the strange stone duo and continued.

"Isn't that sweet?" said the first gargoyle.

"Perhaps, but you forgot to ask if she could sing," said his companion, as they watched our brave little heroine march on.

Amelia took the weird and fantastical statue's advice and eventually came across the outlandishly mystic archway described. A bitter, starless archway, indeed. Though she could not brush off the feeling she was being followed. Light footsteps coming from behind her, yet she could see no one. Tip tap, tip tap, tip tap. How very peculiar.

Beyond the archway she could see the dark, battered old castle overlooking the decrepit remains of this seemingly infinite labyrinth. "Not far now," she thought. That is, until miraculously the walls of the labyrinth transformed in shape and arrangement, preventing the girl from getting closer to the castle. Amelia could have almost cried in frustration. "Hardly fair," she thought.

"Oh, that was just too easy," said The Voice from the darkness. "You are hopeless, child."

"I just want my mother and father back," said Amelia. "Please." The girl looked around hoping this dark presence would finally reveal itself, but once again there was nothing. Even in that respect she felt resentful.

"Your parents are gone, Amelia."

"Liar!" cried Amelia.

"I seldom lie, my pet. However, we could do a deal."

"What?"

"A deal. I'll send your parents back to their primitive little realm in exchange for you."

"Why me?"

"Don't you understand, child? The entire Seen and Unseen universe has conspired to bring you to this world. You're the final element that will change everything, forever. With your help, the Unseen Universe shall be recreated in *my* vision."

"No," said Amelia. She then tried to ignore the wretched haunting voice and ran senselessly through the maze once again. She ran down a cobbled entry, which quickly became narrower and narrower, eventually resulting in a dead end. The girl fell to her knees, sitting in silence; the deathly and dark presence returned. "Go away you... you horrible, evil old witch!" she screamed. "Please!" Through a mixture of fear, frustration and deep personal anguish, the tears poured frantically down the poor girl's pale skin.

"Evil?" said The Voice. "Hardly. Is it evil to bring order to chaos? Is it evil to do what's right for your world? I helped create this realm, I'll be damned if Loren takes that from me."

"Not at the expense of my friends," said the girl.

"Friends? *Friends?!* You don't need those inferior creatures as friends, Amelia. You're not like them. You'll never be like them. We are gods!"

"Then I don't want to be a god!" There was a measured silence and an uneasy tension after Amelia uttered these words to the evil presence that haunted her.

"You won't need to be, my dear. I'll be quite pleased to see you perish in this wretched labyrinth for all eternity instead, forever transfiguring to my own image. None of your 'friends' will ever find you!"

Magically, the walls started to enclose on Amelia and surround her like a windowless prison, with no hint of daylight touching her – or what the realm of the Dark could pass off for daylight, at least. The girl said nothing. What else was there to say? She had lost. No parents, no friends, no hope. Nothing. She felt truly more alone now than ever before.

XXIV

SILENCE filled the cryptic void of the now prison-like labyrinth as Amelia sat in a curled up ball, brooding over her sad and lonely thoughts.

Once she had convinced herself the evil that haunted her had vanished back whence it came, the girl wandered around the endless dungeon once more looking for something, anything, that might point the way to Ulana's fortress, or simply a way out of this chilling darkness. She conjured her lantern like she did back in the depths of the Forgotten Forest to try and make sense of the chamber, but it was no use. She was tired and frustrated, wanting to just fall over.

Suddenly, she heard the sounds of tip and tap. There were those footsteps again from earlier. Tip, tap. Tip, tap. Tip, tap.

"Show yourself!" screamed Amelia. "I'm tired of this."

The footsteps crept around her again. Slowly and methodically.

"A child of the Dark," said the voice from the shadows. A very old and very creaking voice. "I would have waited an eternity for this."

Amelia shuttered in shock. She hesitantly put the lantern up to the dark silhouette to reveal an elderly man with grey, haggard clothes, balding head, a white bandage covering his eyes and a beaten, worn-down walking stick.

The poor girl froze, startled by the stranger's appearance.

"Who... who are you?" she asked.

"I mean no harm," said the old man.

"I'm Amelia Black. What's your name?" she asked politely.

"I have no name. At least, if I did I can't remember it."

The girl examined him closely and thought it would be courteous to summon a comfortable leather chair for the mysterious stranger. A stark contrast to the stone surroundings the man had been used to for quite some time.

"Why are you here?" asked Amelia.

"I helped create this labyrinth, just after The Great War of the Unseen," he explained. "However, because of my foolish loyalty to the Queen, Loren stripped me of my powers, leaving me to wither away in this hell of my own design, forever."

"This queen, who is she? Is she like a voice or a ghost?"

"The King of the Unseen Light defeated the Queen of the Unseen Dark eons ago, banishing her into another existence. However, her presence amongst her followers remains constant. Waiting for the day she returns once more."

"So... she's a ghost?" asked Amelia.

"Not quite," said the blind man, coughing heavily. "The body may decay but the life force, the essence, lives on, waiting for the day when another vessel can sustain her soul. Until that day, she's condemned to drift between dimensions."

"So she wants me so she can possess me?" said Amelia. "No, I can't let that happen."

"As long as you are trapped in this labyrinth, it can't," said the man.

"What do you mean?"

"Only the power of twelve minds can bring her back from the deepest, darkest reaches of The Unseen Universe. The power of the mythical Children of the Dark."

Amelia felt puzzled by this revelation as she had been under the impression that, being the only child of the Black family, only she possessed the power.

"I'm very sorry, sir, but you must be mistaken. I am no 'child of the dark'. I'm only here to save my mother and father from Ulana's castle. Second, there can't be any other children. I have no brothers or sisters or cousins, you see," said Amelia. "Now if you would just tell me how to get out of this place and to the castle, please."

"I'm afraid there is no escape, Ms Black," said the nameless man. "For powerless old creatures such as I, at least. You, however, have limitless power at your fingertips. Use it."

"I don't understand," said Amelia.

"The power of the Unseen Universe is yours to wield! Use it wisely."

Amelia turned away, stared into the silent darkness, closed her eyes... and saw the light.

Just like magic, the entire structure was lit up with the most beautiful and vivid colours, as if succumbing to the most potent of rainbows. It reminded her of the day when she first arrived in the Unseen Universe and looked down on the world of the Light below.

"Wow..." she marvelled. "That's incredible." She turned back to the mysterious stranger but he had already vanished into the unknown, never to be heard from again. She dwelled on it little, as all had finally become clear. With a heavy heart, she knew what she had to do.

She closed her eyes one more time, concentrating all thoughts on the stone structure that imprisoned her. Hush. Then, slowly but surely, the wall began to creak. The creak became a crack. The crack grew and expanded and before you could be given time to think, went faster than the speed of light all around the entire labyrinth. Amelia now had control of the complete structure, and began to shape it in *her* image.

"What are you doing, Amelia?" asked the voice of the Queen. "That's my labyrinth."

Amelia, for the first time ever since arriving in the Dark, ignored the voice of the Queen, shutting her out completely.

"You can't silence me..."

"No more fear," thought Amelia. The girl was tired of playing games with a ghastly, unforgiving maze she could not solve. So, in the interests of fair play, she transformed the long, winding passageways into a direct road leading straight to the castle at the centre of the Dark.

Unfortunately, the monumental unleash of her limitless power had drained the poor girl so, as she limped weakly down the long and widening road.

There in the distance, at the centre of her sights, lay Ulana's castle. Her grand adventure, the friends gained and lost, the horrors inflicted upon her, everything came down to this. What sort of nightmares, mysteries and revelations lay beyond those gates she could not begin to imagine.

A storm started to gather over the dark tower behind the fortress walls. In the distance the sinister, demonic roar of Ulana could be heard. She reminded herself of the words Loren said to her as they boarded *The Blanchard*:

"Don't be afraid. No matter what happens, don't be afraid."

XXV

AMELIA continued walking towards Ulana's castle when she encountered some familiar voices.

"Little girl!" cried the gargoyle with the more commanding and articulate voice. "Are you responsible for this epic redecorating?"

"I'm afraid I am, sir, so sorry," she said, with a look of slight embarrassment on her face.

"Don't be! I was getting sick of that convoluted layout, too difficult if you ask me, we never get any visitors," said the gargoyle in a strangely upbeat and buoyant tone.

"And what would we do if we had visitors, may I ask?" interjected the second gargoyle. "Oh, I know, we'll entertain them with our unrivalled wit, perhaps show them the decaying Giants' Graveyard beyond the hills of yore."

"Quiet, you," said the first gargoyle, and the stone beings continued to argue amongst themselves.

Amelia, however, was in no mood to converse with her chiselled acquaintances at this time and carried on slowly en route to the daunting structure ahead. Part of her thought after all the carnage, near death experiences and complete torment she had been through, that this walk would just go on forever, however never once did she ever consider giving up.

Meanwhile, behind her and a mighty brave distance away, a familiar doorway magically appeared where our remaining heroes Dawson, Sullivan, Boris, Towser and, of course, Sid, finally materialised after their deathly encounter with Zarin Glass.

"The labyrinth will be tough to crack but with some luck we may just do it," said Sullivan as he walked out of the portal. "As you can see it's... it's... a straight line?" The scholar investigated the crew's surroundings.

"You seen a labyrinth before, Boris?" asked Towser.

"Certainly have, Towser..." said Boris.

"Certainly haven't, Boris," said Sullivan, correcting his simple-minded creation. Sullivan inspected the walls and the shattered ground, completely bewildered as to what had happened to the structure.

"A trap, perhaps?" asked Sid.

"Could be," mused Sullivan. "We'll make enquiries."

"Enquiries?" asked Dawson.

"Yes, enquires," said Sullivan. "Stoned creature, what happened here?" he asked one of the gargoyles Amelia had not conversed with earlier.

"Mol," it replied back.

"Excuse me?"

"My name's Mol. Stoned creature indeed, how demeaning," it said.

"Okay, Mol, what happened here?" asked Sullivan. "Where's the labyrinth?"

"Stuff," said Mol.

"Stuff?" asked Sullivan again. "What kind of...stuff?" The man's patience with the grotesquely rude and eroded creature was wearing thin, very quickly. He gave a slight sigh, while wiping the grit and dirt off his ravaged glasses.

"Just stuff. One minute I was looking east, now I'm looking west. Some little girl messing with the furniture. Stupid human."

"Little girl? Amelia," said Dawson.

"Curious," pondered Sullivan. He used his peculiar magnifying glasses as binoculars to see ahead. There was a faint tiny shape in the distance. He increased the magnification once more to see a lonely figure making its way to the dark tower of Ulana's fortress. "It is her!" he cried.

Dawson ran ahead of his companions, jubilant and thankful to see his young employer alive and breathing. He kept screaming her name to attract her attention, but was unfortunately still too far behind.

Amelia approached an enormous grey gate, at the end of the road. At the centre of the gate lay a larger door handle mounted on to a strange demon's head. Amelia, too small to knock it herself, used her powers to move the large rusted knocker with one large...

THUD!

A seismic rapture filled the deathly silence as the shockwave made Amelia fall, landing on her back. The large knocker falls off the demon's head and the girl makes a quick dash to avoid its impact. A bizarre glow emitted from the eyes of the iron demon head.

"WHO REQUESTS ENTRANCE TO THE LAIR OF THE DARK BEAST?"

"Amelia Black!" the girl shouted back.

The strange glowing eyes became fixated on Amelia. The girl felt understandably anxious.

"PROCEED," bellowed the iron creature.

Slowly the large doorway crept open and a horrid stench rushed out. Amelia nearly turned green at the smell. She closed her eyes and imagined all the delightful smells she used to love. She filled her senses with those infamous Christmas dinners Dawson would make every year, the smell of the flowers and outlandish plant life occupying her mother's grand greenhouse. Those wild strawberries, the rustic autumnal apples and the rich, vibrant purple grapes. Oh, and not forgetting those gooey chocolate treats her father would prepare if she was well behaved. Indeed, it was one of Mr Black's rare ventures into the kitchen. Suddenly the poor girl was feeling slightly homesick.

Having blocked out the stench in favour of more desirable aromas, she proceeded through the large, foreboding entrance. Until, that is... no, it couldn't be. She turned her head to see someone running towards her – it was Dawson! She was overjoyed to finally see her most trusted friend and guardian alive after all this time. His clothes were torn, his face bruised and beaten, but that mattered little.

Amelia ran towards Dawson to give him a welcoming hug, but yet again an unwanted presence returned to cause the girl potentially more pain.

"You may have ruined my glorious labyrinth, but I can still do this, child," said the Queen.

Suddenly the ground behind Dawson started to crumble into nothingness. He ran with all his might, the rest of his companions were too far behind at this stage.

"Jump, Dawson!" screamed Amelia. And the courageous butler, with all his strength and will, took a massive leap of faith. Faith which was indeed rewarded as Amelia glided him to safety. The tears poured from the girl as she was reunited with family once more. "You're alive," she wailed in delight. "I knew you would be. I just knew it."

Dawson held back his own tears of relief and joy and just gave an exhausted sigh. "I made a promise," he said. "I swore to your parents I would do everything to protect you. However, it seems like I was the one who needed protecting. Come on, not far now."

"Wait for me!" screamed a tiny voice.

"Sid!" said Amelia.

"You weren't going to enter the creepy, scary, deathly lair without me?!" said the pixie. "I've got a score to settle with this beast."

Meanwhile, Sullivan, Boris and Towser could only watch on as their fellowship of six quickly diminished to three.

"We not going too, boss?" asked Boris.

"No, Boris," said Sullivan. "We're not. It's up to them now. If the girl made it this far practically on her own, with those two there isn't anything she can't achieve."

Sullivan and his mechanical creations exited back they way they entered for the scholar knew their part in this quest was now over. He was reluctant to let his naïve explorers go alone into a chamber of nightmares, but if there was one thing this quest had taught him above all else:

He believed in Amelia Black.

XXVI

THE valiant trio crept cautiously into the foreboding structure. The stone walls were entirely black, whether naturally or through centuries of dirt and muck, Amelia could not decide. One thing was for sure, Dawson was not cleaning it up.

"What... what happened to them?" asked Amelia, pointing above her.

Hanging from above her were the skeletal remains of outlandishly strange creatures of the Unseen Universe she had not encountered in the flesh.

Sid merely passed them off without a compassionate thought, to not get distracted. "They took a wrong turn," he said solemnly. "Though what is that strangely sweet and delicious smell?"

"That was me," said Amelia. "The stench was too horrible so I conjured all the wonderful scents I remembered from back home."

"Oh, you conjured that," said Sid. "I thought you meant conjuring as in... I mean... never mind."

"Now's not the time, Sid," said Dawson.

"I know, I know. I can't help it. I always get a little jokey when I'm feeling nervous," said the pixie.

"I'd never noticed," said Dawson.

The trio continued down the dim lit hall, very anxious. No one had ever made it this far into the Dark alive before. Or at least, no one had ever returned to tell the tale. Dawson walked just ahead of Amelia, looking all around him for clues as to how to navigate through the castle. He came to a heavily gothic archway and suddenly tripped over a stump he failed to see.

"Look out!" screamed Sid, as a giant steel boulder attached to a chain swung down viciously from the ceiling. Dawson ducked but it came back around and nearly smashed into him until Amelia transformed the wrecking ball into merely an inflatable ball. Dawson took a woozy turn as his anxiety heightened.

"This is strange," said Sid.

"What is?" asked Amelia. "There were puzzles and traps before on our way to the Mother's lair."

"Yes, but why would a terrifying beast like Ulana need to make traps for unwelcomed guests? It's one of the most powerful creatures in the Unseen Universe. It can, you know, eat them, smash them, turn them into fairy dust. It just doesn't make sense."

"So it's what? Hiding something?" asked Dawson.

"Not sure," said Sid. "We have to keep moving."

Strangely the next room, of the castle was noticeably more clean and elegant than anything they had previously encountered in the entire Dark realm. Sparse in furniture though it was, the room was brightly lit with chequered flooring similar to a chessboard.

"The decoration in this castle is most inconsistent," thought Dawson out loud as he stood inside the doorway. "Looks like a reception room or ballroom of some sort." He took a few steps further on to one of the black squares when rather abruptly a trap-door opened and *poof!* he was gone.

The walls started to close in on the remaining pair. "Dawson!" cried Amelia. The girl tried to dive in after him but Sid pulled her by the hair away from the pit drenched in darkness.

"Amelia, no!" said Sid. "We have to keep moving. Stay on the white squares."

Sid and Amelia dashed towards the end of the room, escaping from being crushed by yet another trap.

"I can't just leave him, Sid, he's not as knowing of this world as you, nor does he have the strange powers I have," said the girl.

"Perhaps, but never in my, albeit very brief, 124 years in this universe and the next have I met a more courageous and selfless human than your Dawson," said Sid. "When you were lost to us he never stopped believing that you were out there, surviving, and did everything from overcoming

Watchers, neutralising terrifying Snatcher Trees to even defeating the Mother, Zarin Glass, on his own."

Amelia was still unsure.

"It's kind of funny," said Sid.

"What is?" asked Amelia.

"The entire time you were missing, he was feeling the same way," explained Sid. He rested himself on the girl's shoulder and laid a comforting hand of friendship down to try and calm her. "Come on, let's keep going."

A dormant stoned creature blocked the entrance to the next room, at least 30 feet tall holding a large club close to its chest.

"Shh, be very quiet," whispered Sid. "See that thing there? It may look like an ugly statue but really it's an ugly stone troll."

"A *real* stone troll?" said Amelia, marvelling and taking Sid's cautious observation slightly out of context. "I read a book once that said they..."

"Yes, yes, they steal princesses, guard enchanted rings and all that fiddle faddle," said Sid. "These bloody writers in the Seen Universe never care to mention they'll crunch through your bones like butter and afterwards use your flesh as a blanket."

They crept by the troll carefully, trying not to make any sort of sound. The mammoth stone creature huffed and puffed wildly in its sleep, dozily raising its eye once in a while to watch for intruders.

Amelia panicked slightly and tripped causing the stone troll to erupt into life, smashing everything in its path.

"Do something!" cried Sid. "That magical conjuring stuff, quick!"

"I'm trying, but nothing seems to be working," said Amelia.

"Then run," said Sid. "And fast!"

And so the brave pair dashed down a variety of creaking dark passageways, trying their best to lose the troll, but it was no use.

They frantically entered another hall, sparse and similar in design to the first one they encountered.

"Barricade the door!" said Sid. "Just stay calm, Amelia, don't be afraid."

The girl closed the large doors, stood in the centre of the room right under a black chandelier and, as she had done before, closed her eyes and took a deep breath. Whether that made a difference the girl was never sure, but it always gave her a sense that something incredible or, indeed, magical was just around the corner. Over and over again she kept telling herself, "no fear."

The stone troll burst through the doors giving off unsettling grunts and growls while uncouth drool came flooding from its mouth.

"Hideous," thought Sid.

Amelia did not flinch. The troll stopped and roared in her face. "Not nice," she thought. Without a word she let the enormous chandelier come crashing down on the creature's head, shattering it into a million pieces.

Amelia and Sid took a big sigh of relief.

"Come on," said Sid. "Can't be far from Ulana's chamber now."

"It's scared," said Amelia.

"Of a little girl and a pixie?" asked Sid, bemused.

They approached where the stone troll once slept and stared into the long hallway. At the very end lay an epic gate of cast iron dripping with blood.

"No, something else; something worse," said Amelia.

All the while, in a dark, dark dungeon within a dark, dark cellar, Dawson stood silently not knowing if his next breath might be his last and fearing for his young employer once more. Out of the darkness he suddenly heard children's laughter, unsettling whispers and puzzling questions. He thought the Dark had finally broken him and destroyed his sense of reason. Had the Watchers returned, he wondered?

"Stop, please stop," he said, with a hint of fear and hesitation in his voice. He then became startled when a dim light came slowly towards him. He could barely breathe.

"Are you alright, sir?" asked the timid voice. Dawson could not believe his eyes when standing before him was a boy no older than Amelia. "Did the Queen send you?"

"The what?" asked Dawson.

XXVII

UNEXPECTEDLY Dawson found himself surrounded by eleven children — six boys and five girls from what he could gather — completely fixated on him and asking dozens of questions all at once.

"Why are you here?" asked a boy, inquisitively

"Did she send you?" asked a girl, anxiously.

"Get her out of my head, please!" said a boy, irrationally.

"I say we tie him down and hold him ransom in exchange for letting us go home," said another boy, disturbingly. They relentlessly kept talking at him.

Dawson was as perplexed as he had ever been since arriving in the Unseen Universe, but he had been around children long enough to know how to handle them. "Quiet, all of you, this instant!" he yelled.

The collective voices of the children fell to silence.

Dawson's voice softened, "I mean you no harm, I promise. Now, what happened here?"

The children looked awkwardly at each other, almost scared to talk about it.

"What's your name, young sir?" he asked a pale-looking boy with dark hair wearing delicate gold-trimmed glasses and a brown jacket with similarly coloured trousers and a white shirt underneath.

"Theodore, sir," he said. "Theodore Frost." He then proceeded to introduce the butler to the rest of his fellow cellmates. "This is Bella Bixby, Noah Ravenhead, Leo Wolfe, Clarice Redburn, Simon Falco, Isaac Poole, Sabina Galine, Elias and Esther Button and finally, Beatrix Rose."

"Nice to meet you – all of you. My name is Julius E. Dawson," said the butler. "However, you can all just call me Dawson." He sat himself down on the ground for a moment to rest his aching legs. "Now, Master Frost, can you tell me why you're all stuck in the same predicament I am?"

"We're not sure; we were all asleep in our beds, next thing we awoke to find ourselves in this darkness with a voice that wouldn't leave us alone. She did horrible things to us, sir," said Theodore.

"A voice," pondered Dawson. He was still puzzled. "Are there any others?" he asked. "A man and woman by the names Aoibhinn and Antoine?"

"Just us, sir," said Theodore.

Dawson was saddened by this news. Perhaps they were just too late to save his dear friends.

"Okay, does anyone know where the door is so we can escape this treacherous place?" asked Dawson.

"Sometimes a strange monster comes through a giant door made from thin air," said Bella, dressed in slightly ragged clothes with dirty blonde hair and light blue shoes.

"A strange monster? With horrid bat-like wings, piercing green eyes and chilling, dead grey skin?"

"That's the one!" she cried, cowering in fear.

"Ulana," he said. He started walking around searching for something that might cause the door to appear, but it was a futile task. "It's no use, whatever magic the beast is using is beyond my understanding."

"Are you a wizard, Mr Dawson?" screamed Theodore.

"No," said Dawson.

"What about a warlock? An enchanter? A sorcerer?" Leo Wolfe said at lightning speed.

The rest of the children crowded around in excitement asking him to perform all kinds of magical tricks, hoping he was there to save them from impending doom.

"One at a time please, children," said Dawson, tired and frustrated.

"I bet he can save us all with a flick of that pocket watch!" cried Sabina Galine in delight.

"I'd just settle for a scrumptious meal," mused Theodore.

Suddenly Amelia's somewhat endearing enthusiasm for adventure and peril seemed like total bliss to Dawson.

"Well, what exactly are you?" asked the spritely, redheaded and flamboyantly named Noah Ravenhead.

They all hushed in great anticipation for what Dawson had to say.

"A butler," said Dawson. "A gentleman's gentleman to be precise," he continued coolly and proudly, while the children groaned collectively in disappointment.

"How boring..."

"We're doomed..."

"Even a simple party magician would've been impressive, a harmless conjurer of tricks..." said the eldest child, Simon Falco.

"Conjurer of tricks," thought Dawson. "Wait!" he yelled. "Theodore, imagine an apple, a shiny red apple."

The boy was somewhat puzzled by the butler's request, believing their newest cellmate had finally lost his marbles.

"He's lost it, chums!" said Theodore, petrified, convinced that Dawson's hysterics were the last sane act of an imminent madman.

Dawson rolled his eyes, longing for a glass of one of his favourite whiskies, The Reputable Hog, anything to take the edge off this situation.

"Just trust me," he said. "Please."

So Theodore Frost humoured his elder cellmate and a curious silence fell upon the darkness once more as his young peers became mesmerised by Theodore's current actions. He closed his eyes, and with all the best intentions in the world... nothing happened.

"This is just silly, Mr Dawson," said Theodore.

Wails and cries of unity came from his fellow younglings.

"Pfft, magic, who needs it?" and the boy stormed off in a fit of rage and bitter disenchantment.

"I never really believed in this magical imagination nonsense anyway," said Bella.

"Neither did we," said the twins Esther and Elias Button, unnervingly in unison.

Dawson, deep down, felt like a damn fool but managed to keep a calm head with the children. He smiled in amusement, feeling philosophical about the whole thing. "You know, a great man once said to me, 'those who don't believe in magic will never find it'."

The children all laughed at Dawson's ramblings.

"I believe, Mr Dawson," said a timid voice at the back of the small gathering.

They all turned to find little Beatrix Rose. She was the youngest and smallest of an already young and small group. She walked towards Dawson and looked up innocently at him. The child could not have been more than seven years old.

"Just use your imagination, Ms Rose," Dawson said. And the girl did just that.

"I want some hot cocoa," she said.

The rest of the children were so fed up with Dawson's ramblings they did not even see little Beatrix do the improbable {*not* the impossible}.

"Look it! Hot cocoa! Theodore, look it, look it!"

"It has to be some kind of trick the old man is playing on us," said Theodore.

"Old man?" said Dawson, bemused. "Try again, Ms Rose."

And before their very eyes little Beatrix tried again and produced yet another cup of cocoa, then thought to produce ten more for her friends and Dawson. There was a glorious taste of the melting chocolate chunks hitting their deprived taste buds. As a result, this was perhaps the best cup of cocoa the children had ever tasted.

"Excellent. Now, everyone, try to imagine that door. The door through which the horrid beast appears. It could be our only way out of this darkly prison," said Dawson.

Beatrix tried first, conjuring a big red door.

"Great," said Dawson.

"That's not the door!" said Simon. "It looked scarier than that."

The children started arguing amongst themselves. Dawson's patience was stretched thin; if he was to get out of here he had to rely on Amelia.

Speaking of Amelia, she and Sid had meanwhile approached the blood-drenched gate. All was quiet, no curdling screams from the beast nor any nasty creeps or hideous skin-crawling sounds. Just silence.

"So do we... knock?" asked Sid.

Amelia did not respond. She just walked slowly towards the door, which was at least a thousand times the size of her. Reaching the door handle would prove to be a testing task. The blood kept trickling down the door until eventually it ran dry.

"Don't let that scare you, Amelia. These Dark folk just use these needlessly extravagant shock tactics to get attention. Why, once I..."

But before Sid could finish, the door opened thunderously, causing the pixie to zip straight into the girl's pocket. He peeked his minuscule head out, looking slightly pale, "sorry, I don't know what came over me."

Amelia stepped over the threshold into a barren throne room with Ulana nowhere to be seen. "Where are you?" she screamed. "Show yourself!"

A familiar ghastly howl ignited once again and the ground shook furiously as the beast stepped forward from the shadows and called to the girl in a soul shuttering tone:

"NOWHERE TO RUN, CHILD. NO ONE TO SAVE YOU."

XXVIII

THE horrid and twisted beast, Ulana, circled Amelia and Sid menacingly.

"I don't want to fight you," said Amelia calmly. "I just want my family back so I can go home."

"NEVER," said Ulana.

"Enough talking, more fighting, in that case," said Sid. And the brave little pixie threw his tiny spear, no bigger than a toothpick to you or me, right into the eye of the beast. This mattered not to Ulana who was only irritated at best, and clutched the pixie with its bare hand and threw him across the chamber. Sid was horribly wounded to within an inch of his life.

"Sid!" cried Amelia desperately. She knew she could do little to help her tiny friend at this moment in time, as her gaze met that of Ulana's towering over her.

The girl could do little but conjure large objects to stop the monster in its tracks. The eyes of Ulana glowed bright red with rage. Amelia evaded its revolting claws and ran furiously into a large crack in one of the decaying walls of the chamber. The monster tried to pick away at the small opening but it was a futile task. Amelia was feeling incredibly anxious, but not afraid. Not at all.

"YOU CAN'T HIDE IN THERE FOREVER, CHILD," it sneered.

"Yes, I can!" she shouted back. "Please, for the last time, I just came for my parents and my friend. If you give me them, I'll leave and never bother you again."

"THEN YOUR TRIP WAS IN VAIN. YOUR MOTHER AND FATHER ARE NOT HERE!"

Amelia said nothing, ignoring the beast's foul mind games.

"PERHAPS THEY'RE DEAD. PERHAPS THEY JUST LEFT YOU. AFTER ALL, WHY WOULD ANYONE WANT YOU AS THEIR OFFSPRING? SPOILT AND DISGUSTING LITTLE CHILD. JUST LIKE THE REST OF THEM."

Suddenly the walls surrounding the crack Amelia was shielding herself in exploded open, hitting Ulana to the ground. The dust settled and Amelia walked out, angry and in tears.

"Shut up!" she screamed, smashing another large part of the ceiling down on the beast. "Shut up!" she screamed again.

The beast was wounded, trying to stand up and fight back. "YOU KNOW IT'S THE TRUTH."

"Liar!" This time bringing the solid stone ceiling down on the beast. A strange mist started to surround the monster. It was fading from the Unseen Universe. "Let my parents go or I will destroy you," she said.

The beast gave a taunting smile and then roared intensely through the once grand throne room.

"I'll do it," said Amelia, crying profusely.

"SO BE IT."

And the ceiling came down thunderously on the monster, in a collision no one in the Seen or Unseen

Universes would hope to survive. Mist rose from the rubble and into nothingness. Amelia could hear the faintest of whispers. It was her again, she knew it too well.

The Voice whispered to Amelia one last time. "I'll be back for you, child. Make no mistake about that..."

Amelia heeded this chilling warning and looked around at the chaos that was left. This was never what she had wanted. She was not a killer, she was just a little girl who wanted nothing more than her mummy and daddy. A hug, a kiss, someone to tell her everything was going to be alright.

Through the ash and settling dust came a tiny little light. Sid had survived. "Amelia, I..."

The girl said nothing; she had had enough.

Suddenly a strange, large door appeared magically in front of them.

"Yes, the King to save us from this wretched Dark," thought Sid.

Instead, it was a certain butler who appeared from beyond. Dawson rushed over and hugged his dear friend. Seconds later the rest of the children emerged from the door and stood looking at Amelia.

"A friend of yours, Mr Dawson?" asked Theodore Frost curiously.

"Family," he replied.

The strange and peculiar violet mist that surrounded Ulana returned and the dungeon door, the castle, the labyrinth, the mountain, were all starting to vanish out of existence. And unfortunately so were our heroes and their new friends.

"What do we do?" said Sid. "This wasn't my ideal way to go out, not after all this, not after everything we've been through."

The children panicked and Dawson was at a loss. Amelia closed her eyes and imagined yet another door. A simple yet elegant black door with spiralling white panels.

"Everyone, through here," she said.

"Where will this take us?" asked Issac Poole. The children were overwhelmed by their alien surroundings.

"With some luck, hopefully back to the Light," said Amelia. The intensity of the mist increased. "You just have to trust me!"

And with an enormous leap of faith, everyone jumped through the door just as the entire landscape of the Malus Mountains disappeared from the Unseen Universe forever.

All was silent. Amelia lifted her head from the soft dirt to find herself showered in glorious sunlight. Daylight. *The* Light. She had done it. Her hellish nightmare into the blackest reaches of the Unseen Dark was finally over.

Not much was said between our heroes in that moment. While the rest of the children marvelled at their new surroundings, just as Amelia once had, the girl simply rested her head on the lush grass and stared into the crisp ever-changing sky.

In the time it would take to utter a single breath, the King and his faithful subjects, Sullivan, Boris, Towser and Maria and her troop of fairies arrived in a newly conjured incarnation of the heroes' once magnificent ship *The Blanchard* and transported them back to Loren's palace.

Though pleased she had survived her deadly adventure, Amelia felt sad and forlorn knowing she was perhaps too late to save her parents. However, she only needed to look at the loving, caring and good people around her to know she still had a family.

Hours later, back at Loren's palace, Amelia had a personal audience with the King in the Chamber of Thoughts over a very serious matter.

"I am terribly sorry to hear of your haunting, my child. I heard rumours from the underground that her presence had not left this realm, but I could not have foreseen this," he said.

"She was horrible," said Amelia. "It chills me thinking about her."

"Yet here you are, Amelia. You saved your friends and our new guests from the clutches of Ulana. This realm is forever grateful for your bravery," he said. "However, I realise that came at the cost of your parents' lives. I'm not sure how I can ever compensate you for your loss."

Amelia preferred not to speak about her parents. Not at this time and especially not to anyone besides Dawson. "The rest of those children, what will happen to them?" she asked.

"They possess a similar power to yours, with varying differences. They will need to learn how to control it, to harness it for a greater good," he explained. "For that, I hope you will stay and help them in the way others helped you."

Before he let the girl leave, he produced a gold medal that read:

UNRIVALLED BRAVERY IN THE FACE OF CERTAIN DANGER WHILST IN THE DARK

A longwinded title perhaps, but Amelia felt enormously proud to be awarded such an accolade. On the back of the medal was the imprint of Loren's strange and enchanting royal seal, which she had seen scattered throughout the palace many times before.

"Now, Amelia, I do believe there is a celebration in your honour down in Fáfnir Forest. It would be terribly rude if you were not to attend, don't you think?"

Amelia smiled in excitement and guided the King down herself, using one of his trademark teleporting doors.

XXIX

AMELIA emerged from the door to a rapturous parade in her honour; the pixie dust falling from the enchanted forestry glittered like gold, giving the forest an incredibly warm and welcoming radiance. The Sandalwood Trees bowed their head in respect.

Sullivan was the first to approach the girl, his suit now sparkling white and glasses fixed properly. "I knew you could do it, Amelia. Always knew."

"Thank you, Mr Sullivan," she said. She could hear Boris and Towser's ramblings and laughed plentifully.

"Good party, Boris," said Towser.

"Indeed it is, Towser," said Boris.

There was a slight pause between the two mechanical beings.

"...Who's it for?" asked Towser.

"It's for that little girl with the magical powers, Towser," said Boris.

"What little girl, Boris?" asked Tower.

"...No idea, Towser," admitted Boris.

Next to greet the girl was her dearest and most favourite pixie in the entire Seen or Unseen Universe, Sid. "Where in the Dark is my bloody medal?" Before Amelia could feel bad for her award, Sid's stern look became more light-hearted. "I'm kidding, I'm kidding."

"Where's Gargh?" she asked, searching through the crowds for him.

"Oh, I'm sorry, Amelia, he... he didn't make it," said Sid.

Amelia was saddened then lightly smiled and took the medal off, shrinking it down to an appropriate size. "Here, Sid, you deserve it more than I do."

For once the dear pixie was almost speechless.

"Thanks," he said.

"Yeah, not bad, Sidney," said Maria over Sid's shoulder. "For a pixie, I mean." She pecked him on the cheek and giggled as the fairy flew off into the distance.

"Mary, come back! I can make some of my family's Pixitrifle!"

Amelia carried on saying hello to her friends and acquaintances. It reminded her vaguely of home when her parents used to throw extravagant parties. This made her feel a little sad.

Dawson, clean shaven and well dressed once again after his most grim of experiences ploughing through the darkness of the Unseen Universe, approached Amelia and put his comforting arm around her.

"I think they're really gone now," she said.

"I know," said Dawson softly, with a slight tear running down his face. "But wherever they may be, Amelia, they would be so proud of you."

Amelia gave her friend and mentor another hug and looked over at the rest of the children. She was not sure what to say to them. It had been so long since she had had any real friends her own age. That's if these children even chose to be her friends.

"Are they nice, Dawson?" she asked.

"A bit disorientated and overwhelmed by their new surroundings, Ms," said Dawson. "Nevertheless, I feel their hearts are in the right place."

"Well, I suppose we did save them, that's something isn't it?" she pondered. "Who knows what might have happened if we hadn't saved them in time."

"Yes, we did," said Dawson in a curious manner. "Amelia, will you excuse me for one moment?" And with that, Dawson rushed through the crowded festival atmosphere of the forest searching everywhere for the King. He eventually spotted him casually chatting to a couple of noble woodland fauns. "Can I have a moment of your time?" asked Dawson.

"Now isn't the time, Dawson. Perhaps later," said Loren, turning back to his conversation.

The butler grabbed him discreetly by the arm and insisted.

"Alright, shall we go somewhere more private?" And Loren guided Dawson into one of his portals which led into the Chamber of Thoughts that sat like a blank canvas. "Now, good sir, what is all this about?"

"Tell me this, your majesty – were the girl's parents ever trapped in those mountains?" he asked.

"I don't have time for this, Dawson."

"Just answer the bloody question," said Dawson. "Or did you send a harmless child into danger to bring back those children with similar abilities, do your dirty work and kill a horrific beast?"

The King laughed off such a farfetched suggestion.

"You've been reading too many novels of wicked queens and corrupt kings, dear boy," he said.

"I just want the truth," said Dawson defiantly.

"I did what was right for my people," he said. "My hand was forced."

"Your hand was forced? You lied to an innocent child! She could've been killed," said Dawson, angry beyond reason.

"Perhaps, but she did not die, nor did anyone else," said Loren. "And who's to say her parents aren't still somewhere in the Seen or Unseen Universes? I may be powerful, but I, like the rest of my kind, are not all-knowing."

"You're demented. I'm taking Amelia back to our world and you're never to contact her again," said Dawson.

"And you'll tell her what, exactly?" asked the King. "That I lied and her parents weren't really in the Malus Mountains and it was all in vain? Bring up old wounds, then just to add insult to injury, take her back to a world where she's helpless and miserable?" Loren continued to circle Dawson, multiplying his presence and letting his doppelgangers do the rest of the talking. "Here, she can make a difference, do something incredible, have a purpose unlike anything she would ever have thought possible in her old realm."

Dawson never admitted it, but deep down he knew the conniving old king was right. Amelia could not go back, and if she could not go back, neither could he. Nothing to be had for either in the Seen Universe besides an empty old mansion that was once a fountain of love and warmth but now lay reduced to a mausoleum of sadness and regret.

"This..." said Dawson, stopping with an air of defeat in his voice "...is not over."

"If you say so, Dawson."

And so the butler exited through the main door and returned to the celebrations at Fáfnir Forest in honour of his beloved young friend.

Meanwhile back in the Chamber of Thoughts, Loren sat a solitary figure in the blank, windowless room on his elaborate throne. He reflected for a long while, holding the amulet hanging around his neck. His mysterious and coveted amulet. It might seem like a frivolous piece of jewellery only a king would wear but sometimes if you looked closely, and I mean very, very closely, in a certain light, you may see the faintest of figures of a lost, or trapped, man and woman. But only *sometimes*. This is not over indeed, the King thought to himself.

XXX

AFTER the dust had settled upon the realm of the Unseen Universe, no one was ever really sure what had happened on the day Amelia Black slayed the treacherous dark beast known as Ulana, nor of the pain and suffering she faced along the way and thereafter. But it would forever be a day remembered in infamy. She gained a few titles too, from the eclectic creatures scattered throughout the Light and Dark.

In the Dark she would be known under such titles as, 'Amelia the Destroyer' or 'Amelia the Blackhearted,' with an air of respect and fear, I hasten to add. While in the Light she would be regarded as 'Amelia the Dreamer' or 'Amelia the Lightbearer'. However, to a humble few – a former butler, a pixie, a scholar and a king – she would, as ever, be known as little Amelia Black, the kind, curious, wonderful, and now brave soul.

The girl never returned to the majestic mansion in her original realm, and the rest of our world let it pass by unnoticed. Amelia did, however, conjure a modest home in the deepest, safest, most enchanted part of Fáfnir Forest and some might even say she lived happily ever after. For the time being, at least.

Amelia Black will return in...

THE UNSEEN TRIALS

Lightning Source UK Ltd.
Milton Keynes UK
UKOW02f1223260516

275037UK00001B/82/P